THE LOCAL LEGEND OF IRON RIVER

THE LOCAL LEGEND OF IRON RIVER

THE LIAM AND BOO SERIES
BOOK ONE

WILLIAM MIERZEJEWSKI

eBooks2go
Your Author Journey Begins Here

DISCLAIMER

"This is a work of fiction. Unless otherwise indicated, all the names, characters, businesses, places, events and incidents in this book are either the product of the author's imagination or used in a fictitious manner. Any resemblance to actual persons, living or dead, or actual events is purely coincidental."

Quantity Purchases:
Companies, professional groups, clubs, and other organizations may qualify for special terms when ordering quantities of this title. For information, email info@ebooks2go.net, or call (847) 598-1150 ext. 4141.
www.ebooks2go.net

Published in the United States by eBooks2go, Inc.
1827 Walden Office Square, Suite 260, Schaumburg, IL 60173

ISBN: 978-1-5457-5671-3

Library of Congress Cataloging in Publication

TABLE OF CONTENTS

....

CHAPTER 1

....

WAS IT ALL A DREAM?

Fog lifted over the lake as the water cooled from a hot summer day. The fog lifts over the lake almost as a shroud that hides the mysteries of the old mansion across from Liam's family lake house. No one knew its mystery. The full moon would soon rise over the trees into the low-hanging clouds.

Very few people ever truly knew the owner of the mansion. Maybe just a glimpse of him from time to time but only during the day. They saw him taking care of his property and burning old trash and such. Seems odd that someone of his wealth wouldn't simply hire someone to take care of a rather large estate and its surrounding grounds. There was never any movement on the property at night. All the windows and shades were closed, and the house was always fully dark. The only way anyone could see the estate at night was by the moonlight reflecting off the house and the water.

Oftentimes, people would hear the howls of wolves but figured it came from the Ottawa National Forest just down the road. Liam remembers the first time he heard the sounds at night. The lake house would get rather warm during the day, but many nights were very cool. Unlike back home in Chicago, here, they usually left all the windows open at night. The sounds of highway traffic and airplanes from the big city were replaced by the sounds of night creatures. The sounds of the frogs in the grass and the loons on the water mixed with that crisp fresh lake breeze was the perfect recipe for a relaxing night's sleep.

The first night Liam heard the sounds was the night of the sturgeon moon. He remembers hearing the horrific sound of howls coming from outside his bedroom window. It was enough to stir him from his restful sleep. He turned over to see the moon rising over the trees in the woods across from his window. He was able to see it very well from the vantage point of his upper bunk bed. His sister, Boo, was fast asleep alongside their childhood dog, a golden doodle named Lady, in the lower bunk. Lady let out a short noise of suspicion and walked down just below the window. The only continuous light in their bedroom came from a small night-light shaped like a baseball in the far corner. The only other light coming in and out of their bedroom was moonlight coming off the clouds from the bright moon overhead.

Liam's parents always tried to help him with his terrific fear of the dark. Mixed with his fear of the dark were several occurrences of horrific night terrors. As he looked down from the moon and down to the ground, he saw something moving just beyond the tree line. At first, he thought maybe it was the wind, but this movement seemed to be very concentrated around the trees and bushes. This movement continued at a rather fast pace. As the movement went from one side of the trees to another, he could hear other forest creatures scurry for safety. Suddenly, the movement stopped. From there, Liam saw large exhales of breath being released into the cool night air. Then he saw two yellow eyes look in his general direction that seemed to be at least ten feet above the ground! Lady let out a slight whimper and ran back onto the bed. The look of those eyes sent a chill down Liam's spine. Liam felt like he was experiencing a type of paralysis for a moment. He couldn't move. Fear gripped him to his core. He tried to regain his conscious movement. The next moment, he came down from his bunk bed and ran into his parents' room to wake up his dad.

Liam's dad, Will, was always his hero and protector. Will worked as a firefighter back home, so Liam always went to him when he was scared. His dad wasn't happy that Liam woke him up. Liam pulled him by the hand over to his window and told him the story with tears in his eyes. Liam had never been so scared in his life. His night terrors didn't come close to this real nightmare. Will looked outside Liam's window for a brief moment, shook his head, and let out a deep breath of disappointment. He assured Liam that the howls were probably the gray wolves that lived in the national forest. He reminded Liam that there hadn't been a sighting of a gray wolf outside the national forest in some time. He also assured Liam that maybe it was a nightmare, or his eyes were seeing things and his imagination got the best of him. He walked Liam back to bed, tucked him underneath his covers, kissed him good night, and closed the door. Liam didn't sleep another minute that night. He kept his eyes locked out his bedroom window and out toward those woods. Liam knew what he saw, and he saw it when he was just ten years old.

CHAPTER 2

....

NOT A SIGN BUT A STARE

The following morning, Liam woke up with his sister and had breakfast with the family. Breakfast at the lake house was always a full spread complete with eggs, sausage, and usually pancakes or French toast. Later that morning, Liam went with his dad to take their dog, Lady, for a walk. It was a beautiful summer morning.

The skies were clear, the sun was shining, and a cool lakeside breeze felt soothing when it passed along Liam's face. Their walks were usually quiet, pleasant, and peaceful. The walking trail stretched for about a half mile down a curvy two-lane road. On one side of the road were the lake and several lake houses of all sizes, styles, and types of construction. The other side of the road was a section of woods that stretched several miles. At the end of the curvy two-lane road was the beginning of a horse ranch. They walked Lady along the ranch to see the horses and shortly afterward headed back to the house. Liam's father asked, "Did you sleep well last night after our talk?"

Of course Liam lied and said, "Yeah, Dad, I'm fine." Little did Will know Liam didn't sleep another wink.

As they walked along the side of the forestry side of the road, Liam kept his eyes focused on the woods. He looked this way and that way to see if there were any signs of what he saw the night before. To his astonishment, not a sign. No dead animals, large broken branches, or claw marks on the trees. At least that's all he could see from along the street.

The lake house was owned by Liam's grandparents, Tina and Daniel. Liam's grandmother grew up vacationing at a lake house in

Minnesota with her family. Liam's grandparents, his mother, and his Uncle Ryan had very fond memories of those summer trips. The majority of those trips were spent fishing, biking, kayaking, playing water games, having campfires, and making s'mores. During a semiannual family reunion, Liam's grandparents were reunited with an aunt and uncle they hadn't seen in several years. During their conversations, the aunt and uncle mentioned that they owned a lake house in the Upper Peninsula of Michigan in Iron River. The couple was looking to sell the place but sadly couldn't find an interested buyer to purchase it. They were willing to sell it fully furnished and well below the appraised price.

After one trip, Liam's grandparents fell in love with the property and soon after purchased the lake house. It was a lovely lake house complete with two bedrooms, two full bathrooms, a great room that housed the living room, a dining room, and kitchen. The great room's southern wall had very large trapezoid-shaped windows and two sliding glass doors that led to a beautiful deck that faced Sunset Valley Lake. Fifty feet from the end of the deck was a separate cabin and utility shed that housed all of the summer fun essentials. Along the western part of the property, Liam's grandparents placed their fifth-wheel trailer to house extra guests during holiday weekends.

Liam's grandparents would open the lake house just before Memorial Day weekend, and keep it open just before Halloween. Tina and Liam's great-grandfather, Steven, got to enjoy the lake house from time to time. Steven was retired business owner, and Tina was a teacher in the southwest suburbs of Chicago. She enjoyed her summers off from work. Liam's grandfather was a mechanic. He worked hard to provide for and raise his family, and he spent his vacation time and holiday weekends at the lake house.

As for the immediate family, Liam was the oldest to his baby sister, Boo, who was two years younger than he. They live in Chicago, which is quite a far drive from Upper Peninsula, Michigan. His family was very fortunate. Liam's father, Will, worked full time as a firefighter, and his mom, Annie, worked part time as a local librarian. Since her work was part time and the need for inner-city librarians in the summer was extremely low, Annie was able to spend several weeks at the lake house every year. She even volunteered at the Iron River Library to assist with their summer reading and activities program. Liam's father had the misfortune to drive the ten-hour round trip usually by himself. He would make the trip once every few weeks when he was able to string a few days off from work.

The night of Liam's encounter was fortunately their last night for the summer season at the lake house. Because of the parents' work schedule, Liam and Boo wouldn't be able to come back to Iron River until Columbus Day weekend in October. The last day was spent doing laundry, packing bags, and helping the grandparents clean up the house. Annie asked her parents if they didn't mind dropping off their dog, Lady, on their way home. She mentioned to her parents that Will had a surprise for the kids and the dog wouldn't be allowed to attend. Of course, they accepted.

As per usual, before they left for Chicago, the family drove over to the park on the other side of the lake to have a picnic lunch. The plan was to have their lunch, play at the playground for a bit, drive into town for fuel, and hit the road. On the way over to the park, they drove past the old mansion. As they drove past, they saw the older man doing yard work and burning old timber in a large firepit alongside his house. Will, being courteous, waved to the man. The old man didn't reciprocate the courtesy. All he did was stare at the family, especially at Liam. He just gave Liam a cold blank stare almost like Liam was intruding on his privacy. Liam's mom and dad both looked at each other confused.

Will asked Annie, "What the hell was that all about?"

Annie simply shrugged her shoulders and said, "I don't know, and I don't want to know considering that guy's backstory."

Will curiously looked back at Annie and said, "What backstory?"

CHAPTER 3

....

HISTORY BEHIND THE MAN AND THE TOWN

A great deal about Mr. Edwin H. Schubert, the owner of the large mansion across the lake, is a mystery. The mystery extends beyond the families around Sunset Valley Lake to the whole town of Iron River. Iron River is a small town. Approximately three thousand people called Iron River their home. For some, it was a summer/holiday getaway from big city life. Yet for others, Iron River was the only home they ever knew. However, people who saw Iron River as their home would agree it's a place of societal peace and natural beauty. A place where everyone seemed very friendly, pleasant, and would always wave to you as they passed by. For vacationers and seasonal residents who lived the majority of their lives in the inner cities, Iron River was a much-appreciated change of pace. The city and county were originally established in the late nineteenth century. At the time of the establishment, the majority of the area was inhabited by the native Menominee and Ojibwe tribes. Many European settlers flocked to the area in order to work in the iron mines and the logging industry. Around the time of the early Iron River settlers, the Schubert family established their residency.

Mr. Edwin H. Schubert was the descendant of his family's wealth and estate. According to some of the older families in the area, the Schubert family acquired a large amount of wealth in Germany. That wealth was used to purchase a large amount of the land that was to be used for the iron mines and logging industry.

The family quickly built the foundations of their mansion by the lake. Of course, the family went through their share of hardships, and their estate suffered from time to time. The Schubert estate took a huge financial blow during the Great Depression but were able to recur their losses during the economic boom and demand for iron during World War II. The Schubert family continued their allocation of wealth and real estate in the area. During the expansion of the iron mines, the family discovered other natural resources of extreme value. This being salt and traces of silver. This became a steady industry until the final iron mines closed in the late 1970s.

During this time, Edwin H. Schubert was studying and earning his business management degree at Marquette University. The family took great pride in helping the local community schools flourish through charitable donations but made certain that their children, including Edwin, attended the finest private schools. Only a few minor details are still known about Edwin. According to the older families, Edwin was the only survivor left in his family. His brothers both died in his youth. His older brother, Frank, died serving his country as an officer in the Marines in Vietnam. His younger brother, Adam, died in a mysterious hunting accident in a remote stretch of the Ottawa National Forest. Edwin was married for a short while but unfortunately his wife and newborn baby daughter died during a major complication during childbirth. Whispers from the nearby neighbors say, "Do not to ever disturb old Mr. Schubert! He's a retired miserable loner who occasionally goes into town for supplies." He's been known to still hunt for deer and wild turkey in the same area of Ottawa National Forest where his brother died years earlier. But there was no doubt that Edwin was still a very wealthy man. His family name was marked in plaques all around town as a thank you for Edwin's generous charitable contributions.

CHAPTER 4

....

THE GRUESOME SCENE

As the family passed through the long curving road near Sunset Valley Lake, they eventually made their way to Park Street. Park Street went through a small stretch of woods before ending into the local playground and picnic grounds where the family enjoyed their lunch. Their picnic lunch was some of their favorite food—for Liam usually a peanut butter and jelly sandwich, fruit snacks, and a banana. For Boo, she loved her cheese cubes, potato chips, and grapes. Annie usually ate light. Typically, she ate a few Wisconsin beef sticks, fruit, and crackers. Will really enjoyed Annie's homemade chicken salad with his coffee and trail mix. After eating their lunch, they enjoyed the peace and quiet of the playground. No camp groups were scheduled to use it that day. Will and Liam played a little one-on-one basketball while Annie pushed Boo on the swings that overlooked the peaceful beautiful blue waters of the lake and the local beach area.

As Will and Liam finished their basketball game, Boo and Annie were already on their way back to the van. As always, Will let Liam score the final point, gave him a high five, and said with a proud smile, "Good game, Son!" They packed up their picnic supplies, basketball, and headed out from the park and into town before heading home. Sunset Valley Road extended away from the lake and the park down a curvy two-lane road for several miles before ending at Route 2. Route 2 was the main stretch of road that either took travelers into downtown Iron River or down a fifteen-mile stretch of road into the next main town of Crystal Falls.

As Will approached Route 2, the family heard him say, "What the hell is all of this?"

Annie looked up from playing a game on her phone and asked, "What's the problem hon?"

Will replied, "There's an Iron River Police squad car with his lights on and an Iron County sanitation truck with a crew just off the shoulder ahead. Maybe there was an accident or something?"

As he slowed down, Will had a sour look on his face, and Annie just gasped. "What's the matter, Dad?" Liam asked as they approached the scene.

From Liam's vantage point, he sat right behind his dad, and the scene in question was across the road. Will simply said, "Don't worry, buddy. It's nothing really."

As they got closer to the scene of the action, Will slowed down and recognized the officer. Will met him at the local coffee shop a few years back. As first responders, they enjoyed each other's personality and old war stories about being on the job. The officer waved at Will. Will waved back as he rolled down the window and slowed down the van to a stop. "Hey, Will, how are things? Heading home for the summer are you?" the officer said as he tried to make light of the scene next to them.

"Hey, Bobby! Yeah, that's the idea. Family just had a nice lunch and now we are heading into town for some coffee and fuel before hitting the road toward Crystal Falls," Will said. Will looked at Annie with a slight grin. Annie couldn't stand the sight of anything bloody or anything of that nature. Will being a firefighter for so many years would say, "I've have seen it all, kid." Will asked the officer, "What happened here, Bobby?"

Bobby answered, "Hard to say, but basically it's a big old mess. That's why we have the sanitation crew out here. No people were hurt, but a big momma deer and a smaller baby deer got ripped to pieces last night." The officer continued, "We figure maybe one of the black bears from the national forest wandered off from the preserve and maybe into the area."

"You figure maybe one of those big lumber trucks coming through at night could have done it, Bobby?" Will asked.

"That was my first gut reaction to be honest," said Bobby, "but no request for accident investigation reports were filed overnight, and the momma deer has some deep claw marks on her right side. Figure maybe she was trying to protect her young one there unfortunately."

Will looked back at Liam. "Wow, see buddy, maybe you saw a black bear in the woods." Then he turned to address Bobby. Will replies, "My son saw something in the woods last night. I figured his overactive imagination was getting the best of him last night, but maybe he did see something."

Annie chimed in, "Will, it's time to go. I'm starting to smell it in the van, please!"

With a slight laugh from both Will and Bobby, they both said their farewells. Before leaving, Bobby said, "Hey, Will, before you leave town, why don't you stop by my dad's old antique shop. It's just down the road from the coffee house. He has some sports memorabilia in there, and he said he'll give you the family discount."

"Sure thing sounds great, Bobby. Stay safe out there." Will waved and finally said goodbye before Annie got sick from the smell.

Will felt reassured that Liam's story seemed slightly more legitimate, but now he was concerned for the grandparents who were still on the property. "Why don't you call your parents really quick and tell them about what we saw. Figure it's a good idea to stay close to the house and to lock up all the trash and such before someone comes back around for seconds," Will said as he headed closer into town.

Liam thought, *Maybe it was a bear. That would explain a lot.* But then Liam figured, *NO! That still doesn't explain the howling I heard last night.* Liam knew that some bears were in fact very large. He saw them many times in the habitats back home at the Brookfield Zoo. But still something just didn't add up, and Liam's suspicions only grew more after he met Bobby's dad and saw the paintings in his antique shop.

CHAPTER 5

....

THE ANTIQUE SHOP

Will headed west along Route 2, his first stop was the local gas station. Next was the local mom-and-pop coffee shop that roasted their own coffee beans in house. Will loved premium dark roasted coffee, and this particular coffee wasn't easy to get delivered to their home in Chicago unless he paid a lot for shipping. As Will parked the car, he said to Annie, "Hey, hon, why don't you go and check out Bobby's dad's antique shop. I'll be there in a few minutes."

"Sure thing. Maybe I can find something nice for our home décor. I won't spend all of your money." They both laughed and embraced. The family exited the van.

The sight of the old antique shop was simple and typical in this part of the world. It was an old masonry red brick building, two stories high, with a display window on each side and a center glass frame front door that had a sign that read: OPEN. In between the two levels of the building read: "Nick's Local Antiques."

Annie, Liam and Boo walked inside, a little bell rang from the top corner of the door frame. A middle-aged man walked out from the back room. He was a smaller yet athletically built middle-aged man with wrinkles along his forehead. He had short brown and gray hair slightly parted to the side as to hide a bold spot. He wore the local uniform in this part of the world: undershirt under his unbuttoned red flannel shirt, jeans, and an old pair of reading glasses along his neckline. "Good afternoon, ma'am, and welcome. How can I help you?" he said with a kind and welcoming tone.

"Hi, just looking. I promise you my kids won't touch a thing in here without asking for permission first. Isn't that right?" Annie said.

Boo and Liam both nodded their heads with approval.

"Welcome. Name is Nick Rosalie. Beautiful kids," Nick said.

Annie replied, "Thank you. I'm Annie, and this is my son, Liam, and my daughter, Boo."

Nick replied, "Boo, that's an interesting name."

"Well, her real name is Rebecca, but Boo just stuck as a nickname when she was a baby. My husband, Will, knows your son. He's getting coffee from the shop and will be here shortly."

"Will...Will...? Um, oh yeah the firefighter, that's right. Bobby did mention him. You folks live in and around Chicago, right?"

Annie answered, "Yes, that's right; my parents own a place up here. Figure I can look for something festive for our home while my husband can look at some of sports stuff. God knows we don't need any more of that in the house, but he loves it."

"Yes of course. Please take your time and let me know if you need any help or questions answered," Nick said.

As the family looked around, Annie was having a field day looking at all of the old antiques, arts, and crafts that were on display. She especially liked some of the wood carvings that seemed to be handmade with a very culturally festive look to them. There were also several paintings in old frames scattered around the spacious room.

"Hey, Nick?" Annie asked. "Who made all of these? They're beautiful."

Nick said from behind the counter, "Yeah, aren't they nice? Purchased a lot of them years ago from one of the original native tribes in the area. One of the old chiefs of the tribe was a very skilled painter. His pieces are further in the back along the wall."

Liam, Boo, and Annie walked hand in hand with each other through the old shop, especially around the section of some old ceramic fruit and crystal. Liam and Boo knew better. Their parents would say, "If you break it, you buy it from your allowance." As they reached the paintings, Annie took note of this particular painting that resembled the view of the lake from her parents' house. While she looked over it, Liam saw one painting in the back corner just under the shelf that was partially covered by an old sheet. As Liam examined what he could see of the painting. He thought he saw the same pair of yellow eyes that he saw outside his window the night before. The look of those eyes sent a chill down his back, and his neck hairs stood on end. He lifted up the old sheet and saw the entire painting. The painting displayed a hilly wooded area with a cave in the middle next to a body of water. The setting was in the dark of night, and the clouds were illuminated by the bright full moon in the far-left corner of the painting. To the lower-right corner of the painting stood a giant hairy beast with long claws, the head of a wolf, with its mouth fully open and blood coming through the crevices of its pointy teeth. A huge breath of exhaled air pointed toward the moon.

It scared Liam so much that he leaped back a few feet, knocked into the side of the display table, and almost knocked over a big old vase. Annie noticed and stopped the vase's movement before it had time to reach the edge. She exclaimed, "Liam, what did I tell you? Don't touch anything!"

"Sorry, Mom, but-but-but the creature in the painting it's-it's…?"

"It's a werewolf, sonny!" remarked Nick as he walked over toward us. "I forgot to keep that painting in the back so it wouldn't scare anyone. But then I figured maybe someone would want to have it."

"Did that chief you mentioned paint this too?" Annie asked.

"Yes indeed," Nick replied. "His name is Chief Big Bear Toe. He was a great hunter and artist. He made all of these paintings here before he died a few years ago. His family still lives just outside the far corner of the national forest in a reservation. Legend has it, the natives here used to hunt gray wolves and black bears, especially in the fall before the harvest moon for their winter meat and fur. They believed that one their hunters who never returned home was attacked and wounded by an alpha gray wolf and later became a werewolf as a result of his injuries. The painting was supposed to represent something that the old chief witnessed while on a hunt just before the harvest moon deep in his territory. But that's the story anyway. Just an old wives' tale to scare the kids I guess. So sorry if it scared you, Liam."

Liam looked at his mother. Liam could tell she was starting to feel uncomfortable considering the story and the events of today. She looked at the exit, hoping to see Will. Then she looked at her watch saying, "Thank you for time, Mr. Rosalie, but I think we are good for today."

At that moment, the front entrance bell rang, and in walked in Will with his coffee. He gave Annie a kiss on the cheek and said, "Hey, hon, find anything you like? Any cool sports stuff, Liam?"

Annie said nervously, "No, we didn't find much, hon, and we haven't even had a chance to look at the sports stuff yet. Were you successful in getting the coffee you wanted for home?"

Will said with a smile, "Sure did! Even bought a few new roasts to try when we get home. One of them is supposed to have an extra kick of caffeine, which will be convenient for workdays." As he looked around the section of the shop, he saw all of the various paintings scattered around. He, too, saw the painting of the werewolf and said, "These are some interesting paintings. Um…so who made the painting of the werewolf?"

Annie chimed in, "It's a bit of a long story, but I'll tell you about it later. Did you want to look at the sports stuff before we leave?"

"Yeah, sure." Will looked over at Nick. "Any Chicago teams in the shop?"

Nick who was looking down at Liam looked back up toward Will with a smile and said, "Sure do! Lots of cool old stuff from all the Midwest teams. Cubs, White Sox, Bears, Blackhawks, Bulls, Brewers, Red Wings, you name it you should find something you like."

"Great, sounds like a plan. Say, hon, why don't you get the kids ready for the ride home, and I'll be out in a few minutes."

Annie seemed to be done with her visit to the shop, and she was relieved by the idea. As they headed out of the shop, Will headed upstairs toward the sports section. Liam looked back at the painting, and those yellow eyes looked back at him just as they did the night before outside his bedroom window. Liam then looked up at Mr. Rosalie. Mr. Rosalie looked concerned but tried to hide it with a smile and a wave goodbye. Will took a few minutes and found a medium-sized box full of stuff he wanted to buy. Mainly some old baseball bobbleheads, old hockey figures, and a couple of football helmets.

He brought the items downstairs to Nick who exclaimed, "Wow! What did I tell you? You certainly found some stuff you liked."

Will replied happily, "Sure did, this place is great! I would buy more, but my wife gave a one-box limit. Anything else couldn't fit in the van. So how much do I owe you, sir?"

Nick said with a curious look, "Let me see, Bobby said you'll get the family discount I'm sure. Normal price would be one hundred, but let's do fifty. How's that sound?"

Will said gratefully, "Sounds like a plan to me. Thank you, sir."

As Nick packed up the items, he looked at Will curiously and said, "So your boy was a little spooked by the painting over there."

Will looked back at the painting. "Oh, the werewolf. Yeah, he has a very overactive imagination likes all boys do of his age. Plus, he saw something crawling around in the woods across the street from my in-laws' place."

"Is that right?" Nick said with a concerned look on his face.

Will replied, "Oh, he's fine. I talked to Liam and told him that the woods are not safe after dark due to the gray wolves and black bears in the area, but he was safe in the house. The doors will be enough to keep them out. Maybe not a werewolf but that's just a fairy tale."

Nick looked at Will with a tense stare.

Will said, "What the matter?"

Nick said, as he rang up the cash register, "Fairy tales, myths, and legends. They are all stories. Some are simply that. Fairy tales. Other times, the stories have origin stories that are built on some truth."

"What are you saying?" Will asked.

Nick said, "Oh, nothing for you to worry about; you're heading back to big city. Safe travels to you. Be careful on that Route 2. Lots of wildlife along that stretch of road. Take care."

"Thanks again," Will said with a smile as he headed out of the shop.

Liam could see his mother's reaction to the box of things his father had just purchased. Even with those big sunglasses of hers he could still see her rolling her eyes. "Like your father needs any more things in our house. Looks like you made out well, husband," she said with a hint of frustration.

"Better believe it. That Nick seems like an interesting fellow. Definitely has a story to tell." Will got into the driver's seat. "Okay, everyone good to go? No more bathroom breaks until we reach Green Bay. Last chance is now."

They were on their way out of town and back onto Route 2 toward Crystal Falls. Back home for the beginning of the school year. Most years, Liam dreaded leaving the summer lake house. It always meant that he would have to go back home, go clothes shopping, and get all of his school supplies ready. But this year he welcomed it. Liam thought, *Maybe I'll be able to sleep when I get home. Even the sounds of the busy roads, sirens, and airplanes landing at O'Hare Airport won't stop me from getting a good night's sleep.* At least that's what he hoped.

CHAPTER 6

....

THE RIDE HOME

Their ride home was very typical, or so it would seem. They headed toward Crystal Falls and back south through some small towns and forest preserves. Eventually they would make their way to Highway 141 South toward Wausaukee, Wisconsin. There, Will decided to make a quick pit stop at the ice cream shop just alongside the road.

The flavor of the day was mint chocolate chip, which happened to be his favorite. Liam's favorite ice cream was classic vanilla. Boo loved Moose Track or Rocky Road or any ice cream for that matter. Annie really liked strawberry sherbet. After they finished their ice cream, they continued their journey back along Highway 141 South toward Crivitz.

As they got closer to Crivitz, Will said, "Next stop will be in about an hour. We're stopping in Green Bay for lunch. After that, Mom and I have a surprise for you both."

Liam always knew when they got close to Green Bay. From a distance he can see the large Interstate 43 bridge that lifted high in the air over Fox River. As he went over the bridge, he could see a long stretch of Lake Michigan on one side and Lambeau Field on the other. To his surprise, his dad took an exit toward Lambeau Field.

Nearing the field Will said, "Okay, kids, first stop is lunch in town. Next stop is a tour of Lambeau Field, and finally we get to watch the Green Bay Packers during their open practice!" Will loved sports. Even though he was a die-hard Chicago Bears fan, he respected the team pride and tradition of the Green Bay Packers.

Liam would venture to guess that his father's love for sports was transferred down to his sister and himself. He especially loved football. Will played a few years as an offensive and defensive lineman for his high school team. He later played some college football while completing his undergraduate degree and also played for a team sponsored by local first responders. He was a natural athlete, which helped him significantly during the hiring process for the fire department. Most of his family were gifted athletes who also served in various services. Most of Liam's uncles played sports throughout high school, and all of his uncles and his grandfather all served in either the military, police, or fire department. One of his cousins even played football for Notre Dame and later for the NFL for a number of years.

They enjoyed their surprise visit to Lambeau Field. It was such a beautiful place, and Liam was shocked to see the entire Green Bay Packers team practicing at a field next to the stadium. They enjoyed the festivities. Annie didn't seem too amused by the visit, but she was happy to see the enthusiasm from Will, Boo and Liam. They settled back into the van, and Will took the wheel and continued down Interstate 43 toward Milwaukee. As they continued down the road, Boo seemed to drift off into a peaceful sleep. Somewhere in between Sheboygan and Milwaukee Liam followed suit with Boo's plan and quickly fell into a deep sleep.

CHAPTER 7

....

THE DREAM

Liam didn't remember much of his dream, but he remembered trying to run from something chasing him through the woods. It seemed to be a large dark figure of some sort. In his dream, he was walking alone through a deep stretch of woods when a violent storm started to brew out of the west. The Upper Peninsula was known for its natural beauty, but it was also known for its weather—beautiful summers, Pure Michigan autumns, extremely harsh winters, and also severe summer storms that seemed to quickly develop over the Great Lakes and relentlessly unleash their unfiltered furry onto the peninsula. Like most dreams Liam experienced, he tried to run from something but was unable to do so. Basically it's like he's running in slow motion. The sky turned from golden blue to a greenish black. The wildlife seemed to run for cover, not only from the storm but from something else, maybe something worse than the storm itself. Suddenly, there was lightning, thunder, and winds blowing across the land. In front of Liam he saw a cave. He couldn't see anything inside, just an entrance and then pitch blackness. He figured as long as he could get to the cave, he would find shelter from the storm and be safe from the thing that was chasing him. As he worked tirelessly to make it to the entrance of the cave, he heard something behind him growling. The growling was something more than a typical wolf or bear. This was something bigger and much more freighting. Liam stumbled and fell into deep mud. He looked behind and saw the creature, the same creature he saw in the painting with the same glowing yellow eyes he saw outside his bedroom window. He tried to make his way out of the mud, but it was too late! The creature grabbed his leg and started dragging Liam back into the woods. Liam couldn't escape, and now its sharp claws were digging into his skin. The creature picked Liam up further off of the ground and over its head. Liam's eyes and its eyes were now inches from each other. The creature let out a loud roar. The sound echoed through the woods. The teeth were sharp and stained red from a fresh kill. The beast brought Liam closer and then he woke up.

Still thinking he was in the creature's grasp, Liam screamed out at the top of his lungs. Boo woke, up immediately, being startled by the noise. Both Will and Annie were completely startled, and Will almost lost control of the van. Annie screamed, "Liam, Liam! Will, stop the car, stop the car!"

"Okay, okay!" Will said, trying to keep his cool and find a safe place to pull over. Just ahead was an exit for a highway rest area. Will took the exit and kept his composure. He said, "Liam, it's okay, buddy. It's okay. You're safe. I'm pulling over at the exit here!"

They drove along the exit ramp, making it to the parking section and then to a stop. Both Annie and Will hopped out of their seats and rushed over to him. "Liam, Liam! Liam, honey, wake up, wake up!" Annie said as she shook his shoulder.

Liam woke up and looked at both of them in amazement and fear. Liam cried out, "Mom! Dad! What happened? Was it all a dream? Oh, Dad it was terrible! That thing is out there! It's coming for me!"

Will said, "Son! Son! It's okay, buddy. It was all just a bad dream. That's all just a bad dream."

He picked Liam up and held him tight as he began to cry. Boo was always a sympathy crier, so she began to cry as well. Annie walked over to Boo's side of the van and picked her up as well.

After a few minutes, Will took a cool drink and a snack out of their cooler for both Boo and Liam. As Liam and Boo began to calm down, their parents got strapped back into their seats, and they hit the road.

They passed through Milwaukee and saw the stadium where the Milwaukee Brewers played. That was where Liam saw his first Major League baseball game against the Chicago Cubs. Farther down the road they passed through Kenosha, Six Flags Great America, and made their way toward Rosemont and into the city.

They drove down their street, and Liam was happy to see his house and the next-door neighbor, Tim, who was outside watering his yard. Will backed into the driveway, and Liam felt a great sense of relief that he was home and away from the lake house. But then he thought of his grandparents who were still up there. As Will unpacked the van, he said to Annie, "Hey, hon, make sure you message your folks to let them know that they made it home safely."

....

CHAPTER 8

A STRANGE NEIGHBORLY ENCOUNTER

"Hey, Will! How was your trip up to Michigan?" Tim asked. He finished watering his yard and walked over to the shared fence line. Tim was their next-door neighbor. He was a dedicated bachelor who enjoying the single life and the peace and quiet that came with it. He was a middle-aged man who was a professor at one of the universities in the city. He always seemed to be a pleasant, friendly neighbor and a good friend to Will.

"Great! Relaxing but a little eventful toward the end of the trip," Will said, looking at the rest of the family as they walked into the house.

Tim replied, "Oh yeah, what happened?"

Will looked to see that his family was in the house before he began to talk to Tim. Will said in a softer tone, "Well, apparently, Liam thinks he saw a werewolf on the last night in Michigan. During the sturgeon moon."

As Liam entered his bedroom, he opened the window which faced the backyard. Little did Will and Tim know that Liam was still able to listen to their conversation. He crouched down below the windowsill and kept his ears and attention directed on the two adults.

Tim replied with a bit of humor, "You've been allowing him to watch those monster movies with you late at night?"

"No, of course not, but he really thinks he saw something in the woods, and it didn't help when he saw this creepy painting at this antique shop."

"Antique shop?" Tim said. "Find any good sports stuff?"

"Yes indeed. I'll show you what I found later. Cigars tonight during the Sox game?"

Tim said with a smile, "Sure thing! See you then. And I put all of your mail inside on the dining room table."

Will finished his conversation with Tim. Boo went into her room, started to play with her dolls and watched some of her shows on her tablet. Liam could hear his mother talking to his grandmother in Michigan. He tried to overhear the conversation. He thought, *Maybe I can find out more about what happened up there prior to our departure.*

Liam overheard his mother saying, "Yeah, Mom. We are home safe and sound. Not a bad trip home. We had to make a few pit stops, so it took a while. No weather and the construction zones were at a minimum. A little bit of traffic near Milwaukee and around the airport but no biggie. Really? That's a bit odd. When did this happen?" Liam overheard his grandmother speak through the phone for a few minutes. It seemed like a lengthy conversation as Annie replied, "Nope, never met her before. She said she lived where? I see. What was Dad's reaction? Interesting. Yeah, I'll mention it to Will, but after the kids go to bed. Okay, be safe love you. Bye."

Annie made a quick dinner—just a simple frozen pizza in the oven. They finished their meal together and later got ready to go to bed. Annie got the wash ready and laid out clothes for Liam and Boo after they finished their baths. Annie and Will read a couple of stories to Boo before bedtime. Liam was in his room reading a few comics. He used to listen to the stories, but they were mostly geared for Boo since she was the youngest. Because of the events over the last day Will and Annie chose peaceful stories. Definitely nothing about monsters. Annie and Will tucked Boo into her bed. After Annie gave Boo a kiss good night, she walked out of the room and down the stairs toward the kitchen.

Will followed suit. He gave Boo a kiss and said, "Get a good night's sleep, sweetheart, love you."

Boo said, "Hey, Dad?"

"Yeah, honey. What's up?"

"Nothing. I'm good, just wanted to remind you to turn on my night-light before you close the door."

"Sure thing, honey." Will smiled. He did as she asked and then closed the door.

Liam kept his eyes open for a bit, reading his comic books, looking around his room and his comfortable surroundings. He looked at the bedroom window. All he could see was the glowing yellow from the streetlight in his alley. It was a windy night. Liam could hear the wind bouncing off his other window on the south wall. He was startled for a moment when he heard something scratching alongside the window. He got up out of bed and walked over to the window slowly. Liam felt nervous for a moment only to find it was a small branch from the tree next door. Apparently, his next-door neighbors didn't trim their tree over the summer months. He rolled his eyes, walked back to his bed, and slowly drifted off to sleep.

Will headed downstairs to meet up with Annie. Annie was making herself some popcorn and a tall glass of wine. "Consuming a larger amount of vino tonight, hon?" Will said with a smirky smile.

Annie replied, "Been a long day. And now I'm ready to relax, have some wine and popcorn, watch some of our shows on the DVR, and then go to bed."

Will looked concerned. "Anything else going on that I should know about? Anything going on with your parents?"

Annie took a big gulp of wine. "Well, since you mentioned it, my mom and dad got a little spooked today. Something seems a bit off, like something the locals aren't telling my parents."

Even more concerned and looking upstairs to make sure Boo and Liam were still in their rooms, Will said, "What do you mean?"

Annie began her story. "Well, after we left, my dad had to run into town, get some food shopping done and pick up a few materials from the hardware store so he can finish the repairs on the dock. As he went into town, he saw the cleaning crew and the police squad car on the side of the road. Seems like they were just finishing up cleaning up that mess next to Route 2. My dad waved at Bobby and drove along, got his supplies from the food store and hardware store, and headed back home. When he got home, he finished his repairs on the dock while my mom finished cooking dinner. When he finished his repairs, my mom needed a few more minutes before she finished dinner. She asked my dad if he wouldn't mind pulling the weeds and wildflowers that were scattered across the front of the house that faced the road and the woods."

"Of course, Dad being Dad, he didn't mind. He took his shovel and bucket out to the front yard and started pulling weeds. He came across several purple flowers similar to day lilies. He wondered what they were and if he should pull them up. That's when he heard a woman talking to him while his back was turned."

Annie's father jumped in surprise to hear an older woman say very loudly, "I wouldn't do that if I were you, sir!"

Annie's dad in a startled tone said, "I'm sorry do what, ma'am?"

"Oh, I'm sorry," the older woman continued, "where are my manners? Forgive me. I haven't been very sociable lately. The name is Angela Miller. Nice to meet you. I'm your neighbor just down the road."

"This Angela told my dad that she was a retired nurse. Been a nurse for over forty years. My dad's best guess was she was in her early eighties. She's a recent widow. Her husband recently died due to natural causes, and she now spends the majority of her time volunteering at the senior center in Crystal Falls. She also helps her local Catholic church with activities. According to Dad, she's a fifth-generation Iron River resident. Her family were some of the original settlers to the area when the town was first established."

Annie's dad said, "Nice to meet you as well. I'm Daniel, and my wife, Tina, is in the house. We recently purchased this home from some old family members."

Angela replied, "Oh yes I remember the family well. They owned the property for quite a long time. I guess they didn't tell you about those purple flowers and their purpose."

"No they didn't," he questioned.

Angela replied, "You don't want to pull those flowers, dear. They have an intended purpose, and they are harmful to you if you touch them with your bare skin."

"What do you mean?" he asked, puzzled.

"Those plants and flowers there are what we call an Aconitum plant. It's naturally grown around here in these parts. You can point them out quite easily due to the natural purple petals. It's quite poisonous, so you must handle with care. Plus, I would highly recommend keeping it there; it's a deterrent. It's what the elders in my family called wolf's-bane."

"Wolf's-bane?" Annie's dad inquired.

"Yes that's right, wolf's-bane." Angela continued, "Old folklore around here for sure. But it helps deter the wild animals from the national forest from being on your land, especially the wolves. If you take a walk alongside the road, you will notice these plants in front of all the neighbors' properties alongside the road. They come back every year. These plants were planted by my elders generations ago. For protection."

Annie's dad said, "I see, thank you for letting me know. Yeah, my grandson thought he saw something that spooked him last night. According to my daughter, he heard howling and saw something moving around in the woods."

"You don't say." The elderly woman continued, "I heard it too. I expected to hear it last night, especially with the sturgeon moon in full view."

"This is common here?" Annie's dad asked.

With a deep breath and a sigh, Angela replied, "Oh yes, unfortunately. Been that way for a long time. A long time."

Annie's dad noticed a large silver cross hanging from Angela's neck. "That's a beautiful cross you have. Looks like real silver."

"Oh yes. This is one of my most cherished items. And yes it's 100 percent pure silver. A gift from my late mother who passed it on to me. She received it from her mother and so on. It came from one of the original elders of my family who worked in the mines here when the town was first established. They found enough silver in some of those old mines. My elder kept some for himself and his family without informing the old Schubert family bosses. He made it into a cross. Just like the wolf's-bane, it's an extra added protection."

"From what?" Annie's dad asked in disbelief.

Angela replied, "From a lot of things, my dear. A lot of things. It's getting dark soon, and I have to finish my walk. Pleasant evening to you. There's supposed to be another bright moon in full view tonight. If you go outside to look at it, I recommend staying on your property. Good day and a safe night."

"On that note, the older woman walked down the road aways before heading for home."

Annie concluded her story.

"What do your parents think of all of this?" Will asked with concern.

Annie just shrugged her shoulders and said, "I don't know and really don't care right now. Time for wine, popcorn, and my DVR. You watching shows with me or are you going to have a cigar with Tim and watch the ball game?"

Will had a slight smile on his face. "What do you think I'm planning to do?"

"That's what I thought. Have fun with Tim, and before you go to bed please brush your teeth and change your clothes. Love you but I hate that cigar smell."

Will replied, "Gee thanks, love you too."

Will made his way over to Tim's backyard to catch the top of the fifth inning of the ball game. He looked up to the moon and thought, *I'm so glad I'm home. So many weird things coming together at once. Maybe it's all a coincidence. Maybe there's something to Liam's story after all. But I can't tell him that. Don't want to frighten the kid any more than he already has been. Has to be just an old local legend. I'm sure it was just a wild animal, and I'm sure Bobby and the local authorities up there will keep everyone safe. Nothing happens in that town.*

CHAPTER 9

....

UP FOR A HUNT

The following morning at the lake house, Daniel and Tina continued their normal morning routines. Tina got up early to make breakfast, coffee, and read the local paper while Daniel usually slept in later. But when Daniel woke, he was welcomed by the smell of a freshly made breakfast and a fresh pot of coffee just waiting for him. As they both got ready for the day, Tina was looking forward to some peace and quiet after a fun-filled adventure with her grandchildren. Tina loved her time with her daughter, son-in-law, and grandchildren, but now she figured it was a great time to sit by the dock with her coffee and her book and simply enjoy the view. Daniel, who was a busybody by nature, took comfort in working on various chores and tasks in and around the property.

"What's on the agenda today, hon?" Daniel asked Tina.

"Absolutely nothing. I worked hard yesterday cleaning up after the kids. Now it's time to kick back and enjoy my book I've been meaning to read. What about yourself, Daniel?"

Daniel said, "The plan is to cut up some of those old tree limbs and brush away what was damaged after that storm last week."

"Sounds like a good plan, hon." Tina headed toward the dock with her book and coffee.

Daniel was preparing to begin his tasks in the backyard, when Larry made his way onto the dock. Larry was the next-door neighbor to Daniel and Tina. He was a retired Michigan State Trooper who served the state for over twenty-five years. He spent the majority of his career on mainland Michigan working in various task forces.

After a couple of promotions, he saw an opportunity to transfer to the Upper Peninsula of Michigan where he enjoyed fishing, hiking, and hunting for elk and wild turkey. He was an athletic man who took pride in doing Iron Man workouts—a mixture of swimming, biking, and running—in and around the area. Toward the end of his career, he discovered the little lake house next door to Daniel and Tina while he was on a fishing trip with friends. He noticed that the house was for sale and was priced way under market due to a lack of buyers' interest. He saw an opportunity to make his dream of retiring in the Upper Peninsula a reality and soon after purchased the property. Over the last couple of years, Larry has been spending the majority of his summers on Sunset Valley Lake. He spends the winter months nice and warm with his wife in Flagstaff, Arizona. Just after Easter, he and his wife make their way to the Upper Peninsula and stay until just before Thanksgiving so Larry can enjoy the best of the hunting season. One task that Larry was still in the process of completing was the construction and installation of his own dock. In the meantime, Daniel and Tina gratefully shared their dock with him.

"Howdy, neighbors! Seems a little quieter this morning. Annie, Will and the kids make their way back to Chicago?" Larry asked Daniel and Tina as he approach his docked fishing boat.

"Sure did!" Tina said. "Getting a late start to fishing this morning?"

"Oh, indeed," Larry replied. "Slept like a baby last night. Didn't want to wake up. My luck has been consistent, so I figure I'll get out there. Caught a few small-mouth bass, some northern pike, and one wall eye yesterday. Fish fry tonight with the missus, and you're invited!"

Daniel smiled. "Sounds great. Larry, when you have a minute can I talk to you?"

"Sure thing. Let me just get my gear ready and I'll be happy to talk to you."

Within minutes, Larry emerged from his boat. "How can I help you, neighbor?"

Daniel replied, "Have you ever noticed these tall purple-petaled flowers and plants?"

"Sure have. The wife didn't know what to make of them. Figure they're some type of seasonal flower that blooms and just left it alone."

Daniel asked, "So no one ever mentioned what those flowers are or their purpose to you?"

"No, why?" Larry replied.

Daniel said, "I met the old lady, Mrs. Miller, down the block. Apparently, these are poisonous and dangerous if you touch them with your bare skin."

"No way!" Larry commented.

Daniel replied, "Apparently, these are called wolf's-bane flowers."

"Wolf's-bane flowers, like Lon Chaney Jr wolf's-bane flowers?" Larry said in a comedic sort of way.

Daniel continued, "Apparently, they act as a deterrent to the wild animals around here. It all seemed creepy to me. Have you ever seen strange things out in the wilderness around here during your time on the department or during your hunting trips?"

Larry looked puzzled. "Well, I've seen a few things here and there. I have to be careful around some of the hunting grounds that share lines with the Native American Reserve and national forest. That area is much more prone to gray wolf and black bear activity. Much less than here. I had to report on scene to a few hunters getting attacked by wild animals. Some of those scenes were a bit graphic and some fatal, unfortunately."

"Really? Wow! That's unbelievable!"

Larry continued, "Well, it's to be expected from time to time. I handled the initial investigation into some of those cases, but they were quickly pumped up the flagpole to my bosses who worked in the area for several years before my transfer. Why do you ask?"

Daniel replied, "Really just curiosity, and I figured it was important to let you and your wife know about these plants."

"I appreciate that. Tonight a fish fry and tomorrow I head out to the hunting ground for wild turkey. I usually try to use my bow and arrow. Makes it more challenging. Want to come along? I can teach you what I know."

"No thanks," Daniel replied. "Got plenty to do around here before Tina and I head home."

"When are you heading home, Daniel?" Larry asked kindly.

"In about a week." Daniel continued, "I have only a few vacation days left. I'll have Labor Day and Columbus Day weekend off.

Columbus Day weekend is the last planned family weekend before we close the lake house for the season. Tina has to get back so she can get her lesson plans ready for the school year."

"Sounds like a plan." Larry concluded his neighborly conversation, starting up the engine and drifted away from the dock and out towards the open water.

CHAPTER 10

....

THE HUNTER BECOMES THE HUNTED

"Up in the morning to the rising sun. Gonna work all day till the work is done!" Larry sang as he led his morning run up and down the local road before heading off to the hunting grounds.

"How was your run, hon?" Larry's wife, Gabby, asked as she prepared her husband's breakfast.

"Great, hon, pretty easy, just a 5K this morning. Got a lot of hiking to do before lunch," Larry replied cheerfully. "Thanks for making breakfast, smells great. Scrambled eggs with ham, onions, peppers, cheese, and hot sauce. My favorite! I'll need the extra calories to make it to the grounds and set up camp."

Shortly after breakfast, Larry finished packing up his trail pack, camping gear, his bow, cleaning kit, hunting rifle, and just in case of close encounters he carried his standard issue 45 pistol. He kissed Gabby and gave her a big hug. He said with a warm embrace, "Love you, baby. I'll be home in a few days. No cell phone reception after I pass Watersmeet. I'll text you before then to let you know my whereabouts."

Gabby replied softly, "Be careful, my love. Have fun."

Larry threw all of his gear into the back of his pickup truck and headed into town first for fuel. After getting fuel, Larry headed farther west along Route 2 past Iron River. Soon after he entered the Ottawa National Forest. Along a long winding two-lane road, Larry continued to head west until made it to the town of Watersmeet.

Watersmeet was the small town and the last patch of civilization before he entered the deep section of the Porcupine Mountains Wilderness. From Watersmeet, he pulled over briefly to message his wife as he promised and said: "Made it to Watersmeet safe and sound. Off to the wilderness. Wish me luck. Hopefully coming home with a big turkey or two. Love you and see you in a few days." From there, Larry drove further into the wilderness until he got close to Lake Gogebic. Lake Gogebic was the dividing line between the hunting ground in the Porcupine Mountains Wilderness and the Native American reservation just a few miles west of his location.

It was about noon when Larry arrived at his predetermined location. The game plan was to set up camp just north along the reservoir of Lake Gogebic. From there, he would hike a few miles each day in various directions to see if he could find some wild turkey that were usually scattered around the area. Larry planned for three days' worth of food and water. He was a big fan of jambalaya and always made a batch of it before going hunting. A few containers of his chicken and sausage jambalaya were enough filling protein and calories to last him for his trip. If all else failed, and he couldn't find any wild turkey on this trip, the plan was to fish the lake for some more walleye and bring it home for another fish fry.

Larry continued to hike for several miles. He came across an old dirt road and was tucked away from the main trail. Larry had been in this area before, but his curiosity wanted to see where the old road would empty. A half a mile down the road, he came across a barricade that was chained and locked off. There were several signs reading: "No Trespassing Beyond This Point, Hazardous Area, Abandoned Mine Shafts." Larry thought, *I always heard about some old mining shafts in this area. Learn something new every day. Before it gets late I have to make my way back up toward my campsite.*

It was now late afternoon by the time he reached his favorite camping site. As he settled in a nice dry spot for camp, Larry pitched his tent and unpacked the necessities. By then, the day was approaching evening, and he was ready to make dinner over a small camping pot and fire. As he finished his warm bowl of jambalaya, the sun was now setting over the mountains becoming dusk. Over the mountains came an almost completely full moon, similar to the moon just a couple nights ago. This is what's considered a new moon. The noises of nature were always a wave of protection for Larry. As a seasoned camper and hunter, he knew the normal sounds of the evening creatures. The sounds of the loons over the lake, frogs, and insects singing throughout the night continuously let Larry know that no predators were nearby. Of course, if Larry heard the sounds of wolves howling or a growl of a black bear, he knew to be extra vigilant. If this happened, the plan was to let his fire burn and grab his hunting rifle. The temperature was dropping now due to the cool winds coming off of the Great Lakes from the west. The daytime temperature was a steady and humid 85 degrees, but now the heat and humidity were replaced with a chilling wind that even made it difficult to keep his fire steady.

As the moon rose over the mountains and along a sky filled with gazing stars, Larry decided it was time for bed and went into his tent for the night. He slowly drifted off to sleep listening to the gentle sounds of the night just outside his tent.

He was suddenly awakened by the sound of a growl and heavy quick movement from outside his tent. He knew that trouble was close. He could no longer hear the normal sounds of nature. No sounds from the loons, frogs, insects, nothing. Just complete silence. He then heard the howl of a wolf in close range to his camp sight. Larry quickly grabbed his hunting rifle, flashlight, secondary weapon, hunting knife, and ran outside his tent to see if he could spot this creature. He panned the flashlight from one side to another, moving it to the sounds of movement along a tree line. Every time he moved his light toward its direction, whatever it was would move too quickly for him. *"What the hell are you?"* Larry thought as he tried to remain composed and ready to fire his weapon if he had a clear shot.

He heard something approach him quickly from his back side, and he quickly turned, took aim, and fired! But whatever it was moved just in time to avoid a direct shot, just a graze wound along its left shoulder area. The beast struck Larry in the chest with its razor-sharp claws! A fast and steady flow of blood ran down Larry's shirt as he let out a loud scream, fell to the ground, and his hunting rifle tumbled out of reach. While Larry tried to assess the wound and collect some situational awareness, the beast stood over him in full display. "My God! I can't believe it! The legend is true!" Larry said as he lay in paralyzing fright.

There in front of him was the werewolf! It was over ten feet tall with breath that smelled like a rabid dog and two evil yellow eyes staring down at his prey! The beast growled, dribbled and let out a loud howl at the moon. He looked back down at Larry and began to finish off his hunted prey. Blood flowed from Larry's body along the ground until it reached the water of a small branch of the reservoir. No help was coming, and if it were, it was already too late. No one would know of his disappearance for several days.

CHAPTER 11

....

GETTING THE BAND BACK TOGETHER

L iam was home now and getting back into the swing of things. His friends were excited to find out that he finally arrived back to Chicago after his extended stay up north. Most of his friends were the sons and daughters of guys his dad worked with at the fire department and lived in the same neighborhood. Among these friends were Tommy, Timmy, Maddie, Robert, and Ryan.

Tommy and Timmy were a pair of brothers only separated in age by two years. Tommy was the same age as Liam. Both were excellent athletes, and they played baseball together at their local park district. Maddie was the baby sister to Tommy and Timmy. Even though she was a few years younger than Timmy, she always wanted to do whatever her older brothers were doing. She was kind, sociable, and always involved in her Girl Scout Troop. Robert was also the same age as Liam. He was not as athletic as the other lads. Robert was the nerd of the group but always fun with a great sense of humor—often the prankster of the group. He always loved to try to scare them, especially Tommy and Timmy's little sister, Maddie, who was always an easy target. Robert loved his comics and the classic monster movies. Mostly the ones that would air on a local show called Svengoolie that of course he would DVR every week. Both Robert and Liam were involved in a local Cub Scout troop and held the same rank as a Wolf but were getting close to making Bear. Robert was always down to play video games with friends, and on occasion, his friends would return the favor by playing some of his strategy card games. Lastly, there was Ryan. The big kid in the group. He was the same age as Tommy, Robert and Liam but vastly bigger than the other kids in their group. They often joked that he was a descendant of Viking bloodline. The very look of him made you think that he was probably going to be recruited by a Division 1 football team to play utility line. Liam and Ryan played football together in the fall for a local youth football league.

"Hey, Liam, what's up dude? Good to finally talk to you!" Ryan said happily over the phone.

Liam replied, "Yeah, sorry I couldn't talk to you more, but the reception in the Upper Peninsula was horrible."

Ryan continued, "Hey, do you want to meet up with the crew at the park around 4:00 p.m.? It's a nice day today. Not too hot. Everyone would like to see you and play a round of baseball if you're down? Afterward, we've been invited over to Robert's house for pizza and watch Svengoolie. Maybe a sleepover, too, if his parents are cool with it. What do you say?"

"Sure! That would be great! Yeah, I'm sure my parents would be down with it as long as Robert's parents don't mind hosting. Is Robert's dad making his famous homemade pizza?"

"You bet!" said Ryan excitedly.

Robert's dad, Mr. Krazel, was a firehouse cook. Robert's dad and Liam's dad were really close since the beginning of their careers. They worked together for several years with a search and rescue company. Mr. Krazel took a lot of pride in making his homemade thin-crust pizza at the firehouse. He would make the dough from scratch and even mix the sauce together in a perfect blend of spice and sweetness. This of course meant that his pizza was constantly requested at home on the weekends and especially on nights that Robert had his friends over.

It was almost four o'clock when Liam grabbed his cap, glove, sports drink, and backpack and started to tie his shoes. Liam saw his mother and asked, "Hey mom. I'm planning to hang out with my friends at the park, have dinner at Robert's house and maybe sleep over if it's cool?"

"Dinner at Robert's house! Is Mr. Krazel making his homemade pizza tonight?" Annie asked.

"That's the plan."

"I tell you what," Liam's mom replied, "If you bring home a few slices of pizza for us, I have no problem with it."

"I wanna go too!" Boo said, as she came out of the playroom.

"Mom, can I please just go by myself this time? I've been around Boo all summer. I just want to hang out with my friends."

Annie looked at Liam and then looked at Boo and said, "Boo, let your brother go solo this time. You, me, and Dad can make popcorn and have a movie night. You pick the movie."

With that, Boo was happy and ran back into the playroom.

Liam's mom gave him a wink and a smile as she looked at him saying, "Have fun, honey. Enjoy your friends. Tell Mr. Krazel I said hello."

"Thanks, Mom," Liam said. "You know he always makes way too much. Shouldn't be a problem." Liam made my way out the door.

The local park, Dunham, was only a few blocks from home, so Liam put everything he needed in his backpack, hopped onto his bike, and headed toward the park. As he arrived, the whole crew was along the far baseball field next to the playground. Ryan liked to start things off by hitting some long fly balls out to everyone in the outfield. "How's everyone doing?" Liam said excitedly as he arrived to the infield cages.

"What's up, dude, been way too long!" Ryan said, pausing from his batting practice to give Liam a normal fist pump.

"Things are going pretty well. Glad to be home."

"How was your summer vacation up north?" Robert asked, as he headed in from the outfield.

"Not too bad. Glad I'm home though. Believe it or not I actually missed you guys," Liam said jokingly.

"I'm sure!" Tommy said, as he threw the ball to me. "Did you practice your pitching at all while you were up north?"

Liam replied, "Yeah a little bit. My dad would try to set up a nice practice session on days where we didn't do water games."

"Okay, well let's see what you got!" Timmy shouted as he ran up to bat. Timmy continued, "Let's start off as you being the steady pitcher for a bit."

The rest of the late afternoon was spent playing a few rounds of baseball. Letting everyone have a chance to bat. The crew even gave Robert an extended time at the plate since his offensive game was slightly worse than the rest of them.

"What time is your parents expecting us for dinner, Robert?" Liam asked.

Robert replied, "About 6:00 p.m. Dad texted and said he'll put the pies into the oven as soon as we are done at the park."

"Is your dad making the veggie pizza for me?" Maddie asked as she came up to bat.

"Yeah, he said he'll make a small individual pie for you since you're doing the whole vegan thing. He even bought vegan cheese. Whatever the hell that is," Robert said jokingly.

They finished their game, drank their sports drinks under a row of trees next to the playground, and then made their way to Robert's house.

Robert texted his dad: "Leaving the park in a few minutes. We'll be heading home very soon."

CHAPTER 12

....

A LITTLE TOO CLOSE TO HOME

Just about the time the pizzas were rising with their golden crusts in the oven, the crew all pulled up to Robert's house on their bikes. Each of them took turns placing their bikes alongside the side entrance to the house. Robert's house was similar to Liam's. Liam lived in a Cape Cod-style house, which was the typical house in Chicago. Robert lived in a Georgian-style home. It was a small but well-maintained two-story red brick home complete with a pool in the backyard and a decent-sized basement.

"Hey, Dad, we're home. How much longer for the pizzas? I think my guy Ryan here is starving," Robert said. He gave his dad a tackling hug.

Mr. Krazel looked at everyone as they walked up the stairs and said, "Just a few more minutes. I have the sausage and pepperoni pizza and the plain cheese pizza done. Just waiting on the vegan pizza and the tomato basil pie. How was your day? Hey, Liam, good to see you. How was your trip up north?"

Liam replied, "Fun and relaxing for the most part. But a bit eventful."

With raised eyes and curiosity, Mr. Krazel said, "Eventful you say. That's interesting. What was so eventful?"

Liam replied, "Don't really think it's appropriate now, but maybe you can ask my dad when you see him."

"Gotcha. So I shall. Well, it's good to see you. Robert certainly missed you over the summer. He won't admit it though. Why don't you guys wash up and I'll be serving up in a few minutes. You might find something to hold you over in the basement while the pizzas finish."

After washing up and getting some crisp cool water from their water cooler, the crew went down into Robert's basement where Robert's dad already put out some snacks to enjoy while they waited for dinner. Chips, dips, and even some oven-baked tacos were waiting for them on a medium-sized party table. The Krazels were excellent hosts. They loved to see Robert happy and with his friends. Because of this they didn't mind having everyone over from time to time. The Krazels' basement was a remodeled entertainment room complete with a long leather coach, big-screen television, and a huge storage cabinet full of video games. Around the room you could easily figure what Mr. Krazel did for a living and where he grew up as a child. Around the walls, on the shelves of several display cases, and even his personal desk had a vast amount of firefighter memorabilia. The entertainment room also housed sports items from the Detroit Tigers where Mr. Krazel grew up as a kid.

"This certainly hit the spot. Your dad is awesome," Ryan said, finishing up his first plate of yummy snacks and going in for seconds.

"Slow down before you run out of room or, worse yet, don't leave anything for us!" Tommy exclaimed, as he enjoyed the remainder of the tacos on his plate.

"Nice spread, Rob," Maddie said, munching on some tortilla chips and guacamole. "What time does the show start?"

Robert replied, "Oh Svengoolie, yeah that starts at seven. Looking forward to seeing this one. Haven't seen it yet, but the reviews online say it's a classic werewolf movie."

The sounds of the premise of the movie sent a chill down Liam's spine, and he suddenly felt that horrible feeling in the pit of my stomach similar to what you feel when you're falling. "Werewolf movie!" He exclaimed with surprise.

"Yeah, it was released ages ago, but I heard nothing but good things. You okay, dude?" Robert asked with mild concern.

"Yeah, I'm good. My drink went down wrong. I'm fine," Liam replied. He tried to cover up his concern. The conversation just made Liam flash back to all of the things that transpired during his final days in Michigan. Liam thought, *Just be cool. You're home now. Hundreds of miles away from the lake house. All of that stuff whatever it was is behind you now. Just enjoy the time with your friends.*

As Liam finished his thought, he turned to the sound of footsteps coming down the basement stairs. "All right everyone! Come and get it! It's hot and ready! Everyone leave room for pizza?" Mr. Krazel said in his thunderous and cheerful voice.

"Sure!" Ryan said as he did a quick football sprint up the stairs. Everyone made their way up the stairs with their plates. Mr. Krazel always put out a decent spread of food, similar to the way Liam's dad did at home. Liam figured it was the way they served food at the firehouse—buffet style with different stations. The pizza was steaming hot still and cut into small squares. Mr. Krazel stopped at least once a week to a local southside Italian market near his station to pick up all the ingredients to make pizza at home. At the end of the counter there were freshly baked breadsticks, marinara sauce, Parmesan cheese, and cans of soda pop.

The crew all settled in nicely down in the basement with their dinners while they watched the reminder of the afternoon baseball game on TV. At 7:00 p.m., Robert ran over to the TV with the remote and changed it over to Svengoolie. Not too long into the movie they saw the initial transformation of a man into a wolf. Liam was sitting next to Robert, and he was trying to keep his cool. Robert must have noticed that Liam was uneasy. Robert got up from the couch and said, "Commercial? Good. Be back before it starts up again. Need to grab something." Liam figured he was just simply grabbing some more pizza or another can of soda pop. Little did Liam know what he was planning to do.

Robert made his way up to his bedroom closet. In there he housed a large plastic bin full of all his previous Halloween costumes and a collection of masks, one of which was the werewolf costume he wore just a year before. He put on his werewolf mask and claws and ran downstairs just in time for the movie to start again. At this point of the movie, the monster was chasing a poor would-be victim. As Robert made his way stealthily down the stairs, he switched off the lights. That instantly made everyone in the room just a little uneasy. As they got up from the couch that faced the TV, Liam turned to look toward the stairs. That's when Robert jumped up from behind the couch with a screaming roar, and he wrapped his custom claws around Liam's neck!

Liam screamed and wrestled him down to the floor for a moment. Liam was frightened to the point he forgot where he was and thought he was being attacked by the very thing he saw just a few nights prior. Liam screamed and cried for help! Ryan, Tommy, Timmy, and even Maddie jumped onto Robert and pulled him off of Liam. Robert removed the mask and let out a belching laugh! "Gotcha good this time, Liam. I've never seen anyone that scared in my life. Not for real anyway!" Robert appeared unsympathetic and proud.

"That's enough, Rob! You okay, Liam?" Ryan asked as he helped Liam back to his feet.

Liam tried to hide his eyes and wipe away his tears before everyone saw, but it was too late. By then, the lights came back on and Mr. Krazel made a quick dash down the stairs. "What the hell is going on down here! Everyone okay? Sounded like a fight broke out from upstairs!"

"Sorry, Mr. Krazel!" Tommy said. "Yeah, and Robert is sorry too." Tommy glanced over to Robert with disapproval.

"Sorry, Liam. It was only a joke," Robert said, finally noticing how much he upset his friend.

"Liam, do you want me to give a ride home?" Mr. Krazel asked with sympathy.

Liam didn't say anything, just nodded his head in approval, grabbed his belongings, and went upstairs. Liam texted his dad: "Heading home for the night. Mr. Krazel will give me a ride. Be home soon."

Downstairs Liam could hear his friends talking and arguing with Robert in low tones in order to avoid overhearing. He couldn't hear much, but they seemed surprised at Liam's reaction, and they were disappointed with Robert for taking it a little too far. Mr. Krazel walked back into the kitchen with his car keys where Liam was seated. "All set, Liam? We can put your bike in the back of my truck." They exited through the side door.

Moments later, they pulled up to Liam's house where his dad was sitting on the front steps with his coffee and cigar. "Hey, brother! How are things? Glad to be home?" Mr. Krazel said as he exited his truck and shook Will's hand.

"Glad to be home and happy I don't have to make that drive for the rest of the summer. Long ride. Thanks for giving Liam a ride home."

"Sure thing. It was getting late, and I didn't want him to ride home in the dark by himself."

Liam grabbed his bike out of the back of Mr. Krazel's truck, and he walked past his dad with his head down. Liam tried to hide his upset state, but his father knew something was wrong. "Hey, buddy, you all right? Why don't you put your bike in the garage and get ready for bed. I'll be inside in a few minutes," Will said.

Mr. Krazel went back into his truck and gave Will some of the leftover pizza. "Figure this will be a good midnight snack for tonight," Mr. Krazel said.

Will replied with a smile, "Thanks. God knows I don't need the carbs, but I can't pass this up. What happened tonight?"

Mr. Krazel said, "Robert was being a moron and scared Liam while they were watching a monster movie. Robert had one of his masks and claws on and jumped out behind Liam. Gave him a hell of a scare."

"What kind of mask was it?" Will questioned.

Mr. Krazel answered, "I think it was his werewolf mask, you know the one he used last Halloween to go trick-or-treating."

"That will explain it then." Will shook his head.

"Liam mentioned something about his lake house trip was somewhat eventful. He said I should ask you about it. So what happened?" Mr. Krazel questioned.

Will answered, "Liam thought he saw a werewolf outside his bedroom window the night before we left during the full moon."

"Is that right!" Mr. Krazel exclaimed.

Will answered, "That's what he said at least. But there have also been some strange occurrences that happened since then. That certainly doesn't help a young boy's imagination. I'm still making sense of it myself. But anyway, thanks again for dropping him off, brother. Stay safe."

Mr. Krazel shook Will's hand and concluded the conversation with, "Yeah, you too, brother. Be safe. You know, I even heard some of the old wives' tales and legends of werewolves in the UP when I was a young lad growing up in Michigan. Heard about them through friends on a camping trip. One of those spooky tales we told each other while sitting around a campfire. But they're just stories, right? Anyway, have a good night."

Mr. Krazel made a U-turn in and out of the driveway, and Will waved goodbye, finished the last of his cigar, drank the rest of his coffee, and headed into the house. He headed up the stairs to see how Liam was doing. By then, Boo was fast asleep in her room with the door closed. Liam was on his computer in his room. He was looking up stories and legends of werewolves. "Hey, son. You okay? What are you doing?"

CHAPTER 13

....

LOCAL LEGENDS HAVE ORIGINS

Not wanting his dad to see what he was researching, Liam closed his laptop suddenly and said, "Nothing much, just doing some research on a summer project."

"Summer project?" Will questioned. "I don't remember any summer project. Who do you think you're kidding, lad? Let me see!"

Will grabbed Liam's laptop from his hands and opened the screen to see an article and picture regarding the legends of werewolves.

With a deep breath and a sigh Will said, "Buddy, do you want to spend the rest of your summer without getting a good night's sleep? You know this stuff will likely give you nightmares."

"But Dad!" Liam exclaimed. "There has to be something going on up there! How do I begin to explain what I saw, and I know what I saw was real! I'm scared, Dad, and I'm worried about Grandma and Grandpa. They're up there by themselves now! Who will watch out for them!"

Will, being the calm voice of reason, looked at Liam, sat down next to him on the bed, and gave him a big hug. Liam couldn't help it, but he started to cry while his father held him. As Liam sobbed, Will said, "Don't worry about your grandparents, buddy. They've been around for a while. That's why they are called grandparents. Plus, they have Spartan and Lady there to act as their security system." Spartan was the grandparents' large male German shepherd. A loyal and well-mannered dog that always acted like a watchful protector over the family and the property.

"But Dad, do you think that there might be some truth to these legends?" Liam asked, looking up to his father for an answer.

"Well, buddy, that's a hard question to answer. Mr. Krazel mentioned something before he left that he, too, heard about the legends of werewolves in UP Michigan. He heard the story during a camping trip while he was in the scouts."

"Really?" Liam exclaimed.

"That's what he said," Will replied. "You see, buddy, many legends are wrapped in some truth, the history of an area, and the people surrounding it. Usually, the legend is encircled in the history of an area and some unusual circumstances that make the stories more legendary. Here in the Chicagoland area, we have the local ghost stories about Resurrection Mary along Archer Avenue. We also have the old ghostly legends about Bachelor's Grove Cemetery and the haunted Robinson Woods Forest. Heck, even the next-door neighbors are originally from Romania. In their home country, they have the legend of Count Dracula who was a real historical figure, but the vampire origin story was a work of fiction."

"So what do you think I saw, Dad?" Liam asked.

"Honestly, Son, I think you saw some type of wild beast in the woods. They were probably on the hunt during the night since most of the animals are more active at night. Plus, the fact it was nighttime and you couldn't really grasp the size of the animal. And black bears and gray wolves have been seen in the area from time to time. Even Spartan chased a wild gray wolf off the property years ago. But as far as a werewolf, I just think it's a mixture of myth, legend, and my son's overactive imagination. Now, do me a favor and get some sleep. I'm back on duty tomorrow, so I'll see you the following day."

Liam's father tucked him into bed. As he started to walk out of the doorway, he turned off the overhead light and closed the door. Just as in Liam's last night in Michigan, the only light in his room was his alley light and the light coming into his bedroom window from the moon in the night sky. Liam thought of his grandparents as he began to close his eyes. He hoped they were doing okay, and he hoped that his grandfather wasn't sitting out alone by the dock by himself. The typical evenings at the lake house consisted of his grandmother sitting inside the house, having tea, and reading one of her books. His grandfather would usually spend his evenings being a typical night owl. He would make a large fire in his firepit near the water's edge and look up at the stars in the clear Michigan night sky. But then Liam remembered that usually his grandfather would have Spartan sit outside with him in order to warn him of any nightly creatures on the property. The thought of Spartan being there as an extra layer of protection brought him some relief as he settled his thoughts and slowly drifted off into a deep sleep.

CHAPTER 14

....

SOMETHING MUST HAVE HAPPENED!

Something must have happened! It's been three days now, and by the third evening Larry always goes back into Watersmeet to let me know his whereabouts! Plus with the storms off of the lake today he would have definitely packed up and headed back to town if not home. Now I'm getting worried! Gabby thought, as she paced back and forth with her phone in her hand. She continued with her troubling thoughts. *I tried to call a few times now. Each time it goes straight to voice mail. I even left a couple of voice mails to let him know to call me as soon as he gets my messages. What should I do? Maybe call the local police? Maybe they can send someone up there to find him! I would drive up there myself, but God knows I would get lost as soon as I turned off of Route 2. Maybe Daniel and Tina can help me.*

The day was approaching evening in UP Michigan. The weather was very bleak throughout the day. Heavy rain showers that originated off the western Michigan coast have pushed through most of the area throughout the morning and afternoon. But as fast as the showers came through, the weather changed again and left a beautiful evening complete with a major cool-off after several days of hot muggy conditions. At this time, Daniel was busy preparing his dinner over the barbecue grill while Spartan played in the yard with his Frisbee.

Daniel was adding his hot dogs and hamburgers onto the grill when he saw Gabby walk into the yard looking troubled.

Spartan greeted Gabby as he always did by walking over to her with his Frisbee in his mouth. Gabby always enjoyed playing with Spartan. When Daniel saw Gabby walk right past Spartan without acknowledging his presence, he knew that something must be wrong. "What's the matter, Gabby? Everything okay with Larry?" Daniel asked.

Gabby looked up from the ground, looked at her phone again, and said, "Something must be wrong, Daniel. I haven't heard anything from Larry. I think something must have happened to him!" Tears fell from her eyes, and she became choked up. "I think he needs help!"

Hearing the commotion from her lakeside deck, Tina looked up from her book and walked down the stairs toward Gabby and Daniel. "What's going on, Gabby?"

"I don't know! That's the problem. It's been three days, and I haven't heard from Larry. I don't know what to do! I tried to contact him, but his phone goes straight to voice mail. And in a few hours it will be dark. What should I do?"

Tina walked right up the stairs and grabbed her phone. The first person she called was her son-in-law.

"Hey, Mom! How are you and Dad doing up there?" Will asked.

"Will, I need your help. You're good friends with Bobby who works with Iron River Police yes?" Tina questioned.

"Yeah, I guess," Will replied and continued. "He and I talk from time to time, and we always meet up for coffee when I'm in Michigan. Why do you ask?"

Tina answered, "We think something happened to Larry on his hunting trip. We don't know yet, but Gabby can't get ahold of him. Can you send me Bobby's phone number please?"

"Sure thing! Right away. And please let me know what you find out!" Will exclaimed. He immediately texted Tina the phone number.

Within a few minutes of Tina contacting Bobby, a local Iron River Police squad car backed into Gabby's driveway. After completing a few tasks on his mobile terminal and briefly talking on the radio with dispatch, Bobby exited the car and greeted the concern party. "Good evening, folks, how can I help you?" Bobby said as he took out a pen and notepad from his pocket.

Gabby being too upset and unable to talk allowed Tina and Daniel to talk to Bobby on her behalf. "Good evening, Officer," Daniel said.

Bobby quickly replied, "Please call me Bobby. I'm a friend of your son-in-law. What seems to be the trouble?"

Tina answered, "Are you familiar with our neighbor Larry, Gabby's husband?"

"Why yes. In fact, Will introduced me to him one day while we met up for coffee. If I remember correctly, Larry is a retired Michigan State Trooper, yes?" Bobby questioned as he recalled his memories.

"Yes that's correct. Larry went hunting for wild turkey in the wilderness just west of Watersmeet. It's been several days, and Gabby hasn't been able to reach him. We figure maybe you can help," Daniel said.

"Say no more!" Bobby exclaimed. "Let me get on the radio with dispatch and see what we can do. That area is patrolled and monitored by state police. I'll put a request for them to perform a search."

Bobby went back into his squad car and forwarded his request to the state police. After a few minutes, Bobby received a phone call on his cell phone from Iron River Police Headquarters. After concluding his phone call with his superior, Bobby exited the squad car and walked back over to Daniel, Tina, and Gabby.

"Any good news, Bobby?" Daniel questioned.

"I wish I did have good news, but this is information I received from headquarters. Just got off the phone with my superior. My department contacted the state police. According to them, the closest state police vehicle is over an hour away from the wilderness area that you described. Due to the time of day and the unknown road conditions left after the storm, they wouldn't be able to reach the area until after sunset. They said that they'll send out a couple of troopers to search the area first thing tomorrow morning."

"Tomorrow morning! That's not good enough!" Gabby said angrily. "What about a helicopter search or something like that? My husband worked for that department for so many years, and this is the best they can do!"

Bobby shook his head, looked down at the ground, and said, "Ma'am, I'm sorry truly, but this is best thing they can do for now. It doesn't look like it from here, but there's another batch of severe storms hitting the wilderness area now and will head into our area in just a couple of hours. Due to the threat of piloting through the severe storms, the state police don't want to risk the use of one of their helicopters. I know that's not what you want to hear right now. I understand but please let us handle it, and I'll be in contact with you first thing tomorrow."

Bitter, upset, and overwhelmed with concern, Gabby didn't say another word and walked slowly back into her house.

"I wish I could do more, but we simply can't right now," Bobby said as he looked at Tina and Daniel.

"We understand, Bobby. And we are willing to help in any way we can."

"I appreciate that. Please just be with Gabby for the rest of the evening and especially tomorrow if you can. I'll contact her as soon as I hear something."

"Thank you, Bobby, we appreciate everything." Daniel shook Bobby's hand.

Shortly after concluding their conversation, Bobby was back inside his squad car and heading back into town. It was approaching the evening hours now. Daniel decided to sit on his bench at the end of the dock. Across the lake, he could see an older man walking along the mansion grounds. It was old Mr. Schubert. By now, Mr. Schubert was making a moderate-sized fire in his firepit. Daniel simply sat there and watched as Mr. Schubert dumped what appeared to be old clothes and some trash into the fire. Mr. Schubert watched the items turn into ash. After such time Mr. Schubert looked up and across to the other side of the lake where Daniel was sitting. Daniel, being the kind gentleman that he was, waved and smiled at Mr. Schubert. But the old man simply stared at Daniel for a minute. No smile and no wave back. The old man looked back at the smoldering fire, looked up at the sky, and retired back into his house.

At the end of his shift, Bobby stopped by his mother's restaurant where his mother and father both welcomed him a with warm embrace. Bobby's mother, Meg, walked into the back of restaurant toward the kitchen in order to bring out Bobby's freshly made pizza.

"Hey, kid! How was work today?" Nick, Bobby's father, asked as he stood by the front counter.

"Wish it was better. Looks like someone might have disappeared during a hunting trip just west of the wilderness near Watersmeet. The state police are sending a search party first thing in the morning. And what's even more strange, the person in question is a retired state cop and an experienced hunter," said Bobby.

"You don't say?" Nick Rosalie replied.

"Yes. Unfortunately, it looks pretty grim, Dad. His wife called it in. She lives next door to the family from Chicago. If you recall, the dad came by your shop with his family to buy some sports memorabilia."

"Oh yes. Annie and her kids. Little Liam and Boo. Yeah, I remember him for sure," Nick said, scratching his chin.

"Dad, is there something you're not telling me?" Bobby questioned.

Nick replied, "What do you mean?"

"Dad, I always know when you are either really concerned, stressed, or in deep thought when you look down and scratch your chin. I've known you for a while now."

"Oh, it's nothing. Just recalling their visit to the shop is all." Nick looked over Bobby's shoulder and smiled. "Here comes Mom with your dinner, kid."

"What are you boys talking about?" Meg questioned as she handed her son the pizza.

"Not too much, Mom. Just filling in Dad on this possible missing person situation we reported today," Bobby answered.

Nick looked back at his son and said, "You seem tired and hungry, kid. Why don't you make your way home so I can help your mother clean up before these storms roll into town."

Recognizing the look on her husband's face, Meg gave her son a hug and said, "Your father's right. Enjoy your dinner and get some rest. Love you."

Bobby soon after left the restaurant, entered his squad car, and pulled away.

"What is it, Nick?" Meg questioned.

"I don't know, hon. But things are starting to add up in the wrong direction."

"What do you mean?"

"Sturgeon moon a couple of nights ago, the dead deer along Route 2, this possible missing person, and the way that kid looked at the painting, Meg. I saw how he looked at it. He looked at it the way that I looked at it the first time. The first time I saw that…that…"

Meg quickly replied, "Don't even say it, Nick! What happened and what you saw was a long time ago. Plus, that situation has been handled and maintained for quite some time. You know no one wants to remember it let alone talk about it. Even Bobby doesn't know anything about it because it happened when he was a little boy."

"He doesn't remember, he was too young, but I do remember, Meg! I remember the night my little boy saw the same thing that that other little boy saw. I'm just grateful it happened before he was old enough to remember such things!"

Meg placed her hand over her husband's hand, and in a soft calming voice said, "Honey. You did what you had to do in order to protect the family. There are only a few people in this whole town who know the details of that night, and we all agreed to keep it buried in order to protect ourselves and our town. This might all just be a coincidence. That missing person might turn up after these storms clear up."

"I hope you're right, Meg. God I hope you're right." Nick looked to his wife with a sense of comfort.

In the distance they could hear the sounds of thunder and a few flashes of lightning. Nick looked outside to see the storm slowly making its way into town from the west. "Hey, honey. I'll be back a few minutes," Nick said as he started to make his way out the door.

"Where you going, Nick?" Meg questioned.

"Back to the shop. Need to close some windows I left open before its starts raining cats and dogs. Be back in a few." Nick blew his wife a kiss and made his way toward his shop. Nick's antique shop was only a block away from their family restaurant. Small town after all.

Nick entered his shop and closed all of the windows. The flashes of lightning and the sounds of thunder were getting brighter and louder as the minutes passed. Within a few minutes, the shop grew dark from the approaching storm. Nick switched on a light near the front counter. From there, he looked over and saw the light reflecting off the painting of the beast. He walked over to the painting and stared at it as the thunder and lightning continued to move closer toward the town. He looked at the painting and into the beast's monstrous yellow eyes, and said, "I hope Meg is right. God I hope she is right. I don't want to go down this road again. But if I'm right, and I'm afraid that I am, I'm going to need some help. I can't do this alone. I'm too old now. But if you're still out there, I'll be waiting for you. I've waited this long. Something always told me that we didn't finish it then. Too much has been lost and buried already. This time I'll finish it. Finish it forever."

CHAPTER 15

....

SEARCH COMPLETED AND NEGATIVE

The following morning, Bobby was working the morning shift. He left early from home in order to find out how the search was going in the wilderness. It was a beautiful summer morning in Iron River. The sky was clear with a perfect golden blue sky, and the temperature was mild after the storms moved out of the area overnight. Bobby drove down Genesee Street with the windows rolled down enjoying the cool summer breeze. He parked his car in the employee parking lot outside the town hall, which was also police headquarters.

He walked into the building, and he greeted the night-shift desk sergeant. "Morning, Sarge. How was your night?"

"Good. The storms kept all the town idiots in their house. No calls after 2:00 a.m. Everything was nice and quiet just the way I like it," Sergeant Pat Fitzgerald said as he sipped on his coffee while finishing the crossword puzzle. Sergeant Pat Fitzgerald was one of the most senior members of the Iron River Police Department with over twenty-five years of service under his belt. He was a funny, relaxed, easy-going but somewhat disgruntled member of the police department. Pat was looking forward to his retirement, which was scheduled before the holiday season of the current year. Pat was a middle-aged man who joined the department in his early twenties. His plan was to max out his pension at the end of the year and retire in

Arizona. Pat would say, "Had enough of the cold and rain to last me a lifetime. Moving somewhere that's nice and warm all year long."

"Anything come over the state police scanner in regard to that search west of Watersmeet?" Bobby questioned as made himself a cup of coffee.

Pat answered, "Haven't heard much yet, kid. The chief filled me in a bit before he went into his office. Some idiot got lost in the wilderness, and the wife is frantic is what I heard."

"Something like that," Bobby said with a smile. "Actually this guy isn't your typical idiot who maybe got drunk and lost on his hunting trip."

"Oh yeah? How's that?" Pat questioned.

Bobby replied, "This guy is a retired Michigan State Trooper, and from all counts is a well-experienced hunter and outdoorsmen."

"Interesting. Well as soon as I hear something break over the scanner I'll let you know."

Chief Rich Patterson's office door began to open as Bobby started to walk past. "Morning, Chief. How are you, sir?" Bobby greeted his boss.

"Not too bad, Bobby. Not too bad. How are your folks?" the chief questioned.

"Same as always, which is a good thing."

"That's for sure," the chief said. "You were the one who called for that search in the wilderness outside Watersmeet, correct?"

"Yes, sir. I talked to the wife yesterday evening."

"Very good. I've been on the phone with the lads from the state this morning. They have a helicopter on the way to the area along with a small team of state troopers on the ground to have a look. They should be communicating back and forth on the scanner for most of the morning. Why don't you stick around headquarters this morning and listen into the frequency."

"Yes, sir. I'll do just that," Bobby said.

Pat walked over to both him and the chief. "Chief and Bobby, the state police are starting to give reports on the ground if you care to listen." Pat finished the last of his coffee and began eating a fresh donut.

They walked over to the radio and began to hear, "MSP (Michigan State Police) Air 1 to MSP task force 1. Go ahead MSP

Air 1. MSP Air 1 to MSP task force 1. There's a pickup truck just north along the reservoir of Lake Gogebic. It's about one mile from your current location. No movement. Looks like the campsite and the truck have been abandoned. MSP task force 1 to MSP Air 1 message received. We will head into the area and continue our search. MSP Air 1 message received. No heat signature either via our TIC (thermal imaging camera)." Several minutes went by without any further communications.

"Do you think we lost the signal, Pat?" Bobby questioned as he tried to turn up the volume.

"Sometimes we do. The scanner has been having problems since the state police went to a digital system," Pat said. He tried to unplug and restart the scanner.

Chief Patterson gave it a few minutes until it was confirmed that the scanner wasn't working properly. "Don't worry about it, Pat. I've been meaning to order new radio equipment. Finally got the financial approval from the city council. I'll go ahead and order it today. Bobby, why don't you follow me into my office while I contact the state police and find out how the search is going."

"Yes sir," Bobby said as he followed the chief into his office. Bobby looked around the chief's office.

The chief was longtime friends with Bobby's father, Nick. One of the pictures in the chief's office showed the chief as a young man in a group photo during a hunting trip. One of the other young men in the photo was Bobby's father. The chief had been a member of the department longer than Sergeant Pat. While Pat talked half his shift away about how much he wanted to retire, the chief never showed any interests in slowing down. The chief was going to be forced into retirement within a few years, but until then, he remained a prominent and powerful figure within the Iron River community.

The chief was sitting behind his desk while he talked with one of Michigan State Police representatives. "Hey, this is Chief Patterson up in Iron River. We lost our signal from our scanner. Any other information on that search? What did you find? Large claw marks and the campsite was damaged. Nobody wandering around. And of course no bodies. Nothing. Well, that's a shame. You'll continue the search for a little longer. What about a water search along the reservoir? I see. I understand. Very well," the chief concluded and looked over to Bobby.

"So, I'm guessing no good news, Chief?" Bobby questioned.

The chief answered, "Well, this is what I was told. They performed a grid search of the area. About a five-mile radius from the campsite. Some large claw marks in the tent. Maybe a large black bear they think. Nobody found though. No body. No blood. Hell, not even the man's weapons. All of that is gone. They plan to do a small search along the shallow ends of the reservoir, but that's it for now. The reservoir is so deep it would be nearly impossible to search the whole thing. Especially with the storms last night the tide could have carried his body out to sea for all we know. So you don't need to worry about contacting the wife. That's a huge burden, especially for a young officer like yourself. I have some experience in these sorts of things. I'll contact the wife myself. I'll drive out to their house after the state police dive team completes their search along the water. By then, the state will determine that the search has been complete and negative. Unfortunately, until he is found alive or dead, his status will remain missing until otherwise determined."

CHAPTER 16

....

PLANNING THE NEXT TRIP

"Good morning, everyone. How's was your night? Did everyone sleep well?" Will asked after another long shift at the firehouse.

Boo and Liam were having breakfast in the dining room. They always enjoyed running up to their dad and giving him a big hug after he came home from shift. "I sure did, and I think Boo slept well too," Liam said with warm embrace and a smile.

"Is that right, Boo?" My dad questioned.

Boo replied with a simple approval of yes.

"How was your night, Dad? Were you able to get any sleep yourself?" Liam questioned as he looked up to his tired eyes.

With a laugh Will replied, "Are you kidding? Of course not. It's still the end of summer. Hot, humid, and dry nights are never a good combination. We were out most of the night. Plus, I had watch last night, so either I was out on calls or sitting at the watch desk."

"Are you still planning to take us to the baseball game later today?" Liam questioned. He had hoped his father wasn't too tired.

His father replied, "Of course, kid. Game starts at 1:00 p.m. Got us the family pass, so lunch is hot dogs and drinks. We want to get down there around the time the gates open so we can get the free bobblehead giveaway. So that leaves me with a couple of hours to get some sleep. No worries."

Annie walked into the room to greet Will. "Hey, hon. From what I heard in the other room, sounds like you had another fun night." And with that she gave him a kiss.

67

"Please don't remind me. I'm trying to forget it. No fires. Just a lot of 'down from the unknown' outside the local bars. Already got my shower before I left work. I'll go lie down before the game."

"Before you do that, hon, can you walk with me outside? I want to show you something in the garden," Annie said, concerned.

"Okay sure, sounds good. Hey, kids, I'm going outside with Mom for a few. Why don't you finish your breakfast." Will and Annie began to walk outside toward the backyard. "What do you want to show me? Did those damn rabbits get into my green peppers again?" Will questioned as he looked around the garden.

"No. I didn't want the kids to overhear what I need to say."

"What's the matter, hon?" Will questioned.

"It's about Larry!" Annie exclaimed.

"Larry? The next-door neighbor near your folks? Did something happen to him?"

Annie replied, "We don't know. Last night, I talked to my mother on the phone after the kids went to bed. Bobby helped set up a search with the state police. They searched the area. Search teams, helicopters, dive team, you name it. They found his truck and his campsite but no Larry. The Iron River Police Chief went to Larry's house last night to talk to Gabby. My parents were with Gabby when the chief arrived. The chief told Gabby that officially her husband is missing and the search has been complete and negative thus far."

Will, stunned by the news, said, "I can't believe it! Larry! I feel so bad for his family. What is Gabby's family planning to do? What should we tell the kids?"

Annie answered, "Gabby has her daughter and her two grandkids arriving within the next day or two. They are driving in from Minnesota. They plan to stay with Gabby until otherwise. I'll plan on saying nothing to the kids until we know more about what happened. My mom mentioned that it's possible that Larry fell victim to a bear attack judging from the evidence at the campsite. Sorry to break this to you now, but I wanted us to be on the same page. Why don't you get some sleep if you can. Liam and Boo are both looking forward to the baseball game."

Will replied, "Sounds like a plan. Even an hour of sleep and some really good coffee will help me get through the rest of the day.

Are we still planning to go back up to UP Michigan for Columbus Day weekend?"

"That's the plan, for now at least. You know that's the last holiday weekend with the family before my parents close up the lake house for the season. Plus, you're on vacation that weekend and they'll need your help taking the dock out of the water."

"Okay. Well, on that note let's get back inside and I'll get some sleep while I still can. Let's play it cool and enjoy the day with the kids. Their summer will be over in a matter of a few days," Will said as he walked hand in hand with Annie back into the house.

Within a few hours, the family were loading up the car and heading to the southside of Chicago to see the White Sox take on the Oakland Athletics. Even though they lived on the northside of the city, Will preferred the White Sox over the Cubs. Will's grandparents and most of my great-uncles were born and raised on the southside of Chicago in and around Garfield Ridge. Because of this, Will grew up in a White Sox home.

It was a perfect day for a ball game. There were partly cloudy skies, dry with low humidity, and a calm cool breeze coming off the lake. Will liked to sit on the first-base side in order to have the shade throughout the game. Since Willl drove fire trucks in and around the city, he knew some of the shortcuts to get to the stadium while avoiding most the crowds. They arrived just in time. As the gates opened, they were already in line, and each member of the family received their complimentary bobbleheads. The game was tight until a walk-off home run won the game, and the White Sox won! On the way home, they picked up some take-out for dinner. Breaded steak sandwiches and fries were the perfect end to another summer day. Liam and Boo had no idea what was going on at the lake house. Even if they did know, nothing could have prepared them for what happened during Columbus Day weekend.

CHAPTER 17

....

BACK TO SCHOOL KIDS

Some time passed since Larry's disappearance. By now, Gabby had lost hope that her husband's body would be found, let alone be alive. Gabby's daughter and her two grandchildren stayed with her. Due to the unusual family circumstances, the school for Gabby's grandchildren allowed them to attend remote learning from Iron River. Gabby had Wi-Fi in her home, but the signal would fade due to the remote location. Occasionally, the grandchildren had to go to the Iron River Library in order to use their free internet. Since Annie helped with volunteer work at the library over summer, she was able to secure a private study room for Gabby's grandchildren.

School started up once again. Boo hated the beginning of another school year. She was entering third grade as Liam was entering fifth grade. Liam was one of the weird kids. He looked forward to the beginning of another school year. He always loved shopping for a new school wardrobe, getting fresh school supplies, and having a new backpack and notebooks. He always made a promise to himself every year that he would keep all his supplies and notebooks clean and organized throughout the school year. But of course, he would always forget that promise by the beginning of the holiday season. By then, he was busy juggling workloads between schoolwork and going to sports practice.

Come to think of it, Boo always enjoyed shopping for her new school wardrobe. Ever since she was old enough to walk, she was piecing together outfits and making herself fashionable. This no doubt made it fun for her and her mom to shop. Of course, Will didn't want any part of it. Liam remembered early on that his dad spent hours sitting alone in a chair inside a clothing store while Boo tried on different clothes. This duty fell to their mom over the last couple of years, which of course she didn't mind.

The beginning of the school year also meant the beginning of football season with the local team. Liam could always count on Ryan to be there with him at practice. Ryan was a gifted offensive and defensive lineman. Liam was faster than he was strong. Liam's talents were spent as a running back and defensive cornerback. They would often hope that their friends Tommy and Robert would be in their homerooms together. It was always fun arriving at school on the first day. Liam enjoyed finding his homeroom and seeing if his buddies were in class with him. Liam was happy to find out that Robert and Ryan were in his homeroom with him. They were especially happy to find out that their homeroom teacher was Mr. Melone, who was also their football and baseball coach. Mr. Melone was a kind, easy-going teacher with a great sense of humor. Somehow, he could make even the most boring of subjects fun to learn. But they could tell that Mr. Melone's favorite subjects were history and science. He would sometimes help the science lab teacher if he had the period off from instruction. He paid strict attention to detail when it came to the science lab by making sure all his students knew the scientific method of research, which included their theory, hypothesis, procedure, data collection, and calculated conclusion.

Class always started off with Mr. Melone exclaiming, "Have a seat by the bell one time, let's go!"

Ryan who was always the class clown would ask Mr. Melone the same question every day. "So, Mr. Melone, what are we going to do today?"

Mr. Melone answered, "Today is going to be a great day. Today we get to sit around and do nothing! Just chill, watch a movie, play some video games, get some takeout, and play with our phones until we go home. How's that sound?"

The students would reply, "That sounds amazing!"

Mr. Melone jokingly replied, "Nope, sorry, I forget we are planning to do that on the second Tuesday of next week. Sorry guys! Today we got some work to do. Now, pass up your homework and open your books to…"

That's how their day would start. Tommy was in a different homeroom across the hall. They were a bit bummed out that they didn't get to hang out with him throughout the day. Fortunately, they would be able to socialize together in the hallway and during the lunch period. Timmy was in the same homeroom as Boo. Maddie was another grade below Boo and Timmy. Liam didn't get to see Boo much during the school day since they were on different floors and their lunch schedules were different.

Robert sat down next to Ryan and Liam during lunch. Liam heard Ryan kick Robert from under the table and say, "Hey, Robert. Don't you have something to say to our friend here?"

Robert said, "Hey, Liam. Sorry that I scared you with that werewolf stunt in the basement. It was mean. Ryan and the rest of crew didn't like seeing you so upset. Buds?"

Liam answered, "Of course buds, bro. No hard feelings."

Robert questioned, "So, what was the big deal that night anyway? Were you that afraid of the movie?"

Liam answered, "Don't worry about it. I was just startled by the lights going off and something jumping out at me from behind the couch. Just forget it, dude."

Ryan interjected saying, "Yeah, Robert, just forget it and move on, bro. So onward to this weekend. Are you coming to our game, Robert? We are playing the Falcons. Should be a good matchup."

Robert replied, "I'll go to your silly football game as long as you both keep your promise of playing video games and going to the comic book store with me after the game."

Liam said, "I'm game but no scary movies please."

Robert replied, "Oh come on, man! There's supposed to be another good…"

Ryan exclaimed, "Video games and comics were the deal, Robert. We could be up for a regular old-fashioned comedy movie if your dad makes his famous pizza again."

Robert answered, "I'll check to see if my dad will be home from work. I'm sure it won't be a problem. Deal?"

Ryan and Liam looked at each other, smiled, and then looked back to Robert as they said, "Deal!"

The rest of September fell into the same old schedule. School during the week, football practice in the late afternoon, homework in the evening, game day on Saturday, church on Sundays, and hanging out with friends whenever time allowed. The rigorous schedule was good for Liam. It helped him sleep better at night and forget about what happened at the lake house. Just before Labor Day weekend, his grandparents made their way home from Michigan without incident. Daniel used almost all of his vacation time, and Tina had to get ready for another school year. They stopped by the house on their way home to drop off Lady after her extended vacation. Liam and Boo were happy to have their trusty dog back home. No one would be back up to the lake house until Columbus Day Weekend for the final weekend getaway for the season. At this particular moment, only the grown-ups knew about Larry's unusual disappearance.

CHAPTER 18

....

CAN I COME WITH YOU?

This particular Friday morning started off like any other. It was the end of another week of school and the beginning of Columbus Day weekend. Will arrived home from work early in the morning. Boo and Liam enjoyed their breakfast. Liam preferred to have cheesy eggs and french toast while Boo enjoyed her cereal and a banana. The coffee was brewing, and the parents were getting ready for the day. "Hey, Dad, are you going to drop us off at school?" Liam questioned, as his dad walked into the dining room.

Will answered, "Of course. After I drop you and Boo off at school, I have to do a food run and get some other supplies before we leave for the lake house."

Liam questioned, "What time are we leaving Dad?"

Will replied, "As soon as you get home from school, kids. I would like to get north of Milwaukee before the evening rush hour. If we leave on time, we should arrive in Michigan by 10:00 p.m. Do you have your bags packed?"

Boo and Liam both answered, "Yes."

After they finished breakfast, they gathered their backpacks and headed outside to the family van. "All buckled in, kids? Safety first," Will said as he put the key into the ignition.

"Sure am, Dad. Good to go," Liam said as he looked over to make sure Boo was secured as well. As Will drove Liam asked, "Hey, Dad. Quick question. A couple of my buddies showed interest in coming up with us this weekend. Do you think it would be okay for them to come?"

Will replied, "Which friends are interested in coming, bud?"

Liam answered, "Just Ryan and Robert. They've never been there, and they both hear me talking about it all the time."

Will was silent for a couple of minutes and then said, "Well, I suppose it will be okay. I'll have to talk to their parents directly before the end of the school day. Tell you what. You have to keep your cell phones in your lockers, right?"

Liam answered, "Yeah that's right. We're allowed to go to our lockers and use them at lunch and at the end of day."

Will replied, "Check your phones by lunchtime. I should have a definite answer for you then. That way you can tell your friends. My only request is they go straight home, pack, and be ready by 3:30 p.m. Understood?"

Liam answered with enthusiasm, "Yeah! Understood, Dad. That will do for sure!"

Will dropped them off, and Liam walked with Boo to her class before heading to his section of the building. Their elementary school was rather large inner-city school. The school itself held students from kindergarten up to eighth grade. As Liam walked onto his floor of the school, he saw Ryan and Robert waiting for him near his locker. Ryan was sporting one of his many Bears football jerseys. Ryan ran up to Liam in a charge and tried to tackle him into the lockers. Liam did a quick swim move and peeled off of him just in time. "You have to work on your foot work, bro," Liam said jokingly to Ryan.

Ryan replied, "Yeah, yeah, not all of us are as quick as you, Liam. Some of us are a bit larger and stronger."

Robert grinned at both of them as he stood near their classroom doorway. He was wearing his typical jeans and monster T-shirt. This T-shirt in particular was a picture of Frankenstein. He walked over Liam and Ryan asked, "So, did you ask your parents about this weekend?"

Liam answered, "Sure did. My dad said he'll contact your folks today before the end of school to make sure it's cool."

Ryan said excitedly, "Talked to my dad already. He's really cool with it. He said having me away will give him some quality time with Mom. Whatever that means. Plus, there's no football game this weekend due to the holiday."

Liam turned and looked at Robert and asked, "What did your parents say?"

Robert looked down to the ground with a grin and said, "I forgot to ask them. But my dad and your dad are tight, so I'm sure it won't be a problem. Hopefully your dad will ask my dad before my old man walks into my room and sees my sleeping bag and duffle bag packed. He'll probably think I'll run away or something. When will we know if we are good to go?"

Liam answered, "My dad said he'll text me yay or nay before the end of the school day."

"Sounds like a plan. Looking forward to a change of scenery. Any good-looking girls up there?" Ryan questioned. He tried to fix his hair off a reflection from the classroom door window.

"None that I've seen. At least this far into the season. Over the peak of summer there's a few cute girls here and there, but I guess you'll have to wait and see."

They finished their conversation, and the first-period bell rang across the hallways and into the classrooms. Liam quickly put his cell phone into his locker and walked to class with his buds. Even though Liam physically was in class, his mind was wondering if his friends would be allowed to come up north with him.

"Hey, brother. What's going on? Oh, nothing much. Listen, the family and I are heading up north this weekend, and Liam was wondering if Robert can come along with us?" Will asked Mr. Krazel. "Yeah, I guess he forget to mention it you, but if it's cool I can pick up Robert around 3:30 p.m. I'll have him home no later than 8:00 p.m. on Monday evening. Columbus Day that's right. No, I don't have to work. I started vacation today. Yeah, you know the wife will have more work for me at home than I do at work. It's not a problem. There's plenty of room. Yup, I have to go up there anyway to help close up the place for the season. Okay, sounds good. Liam will be thrilled. I've already talked to Ryan's dad as he's cool with it too. Great, I'll text Liam and let him know the good news. Thanks, brother. Stay safe. Bye." Will concluded his conversation with Mr. Krazel and then texted Liam.

At lunch, Liam walked over to his locker and checked his cell phone. He hoped to see a message from his father, and it was certainly there waiting for him. The message from his dad read:

"Ryan and Robert are good to go for this weekend. Talked to their parents. Van leaves for UP Michigan at 3:30 p.m. You're welcome."

Liam ran up to his buds who were already in the lunchroom. Ryan was eating a healthy portion of chicken tenders and fries while Robert chewed on his sub sandwich and chips. "Guys! Guys! Guys!" Liam exclaimed as he ran up to their lunch table.

"What? What? What?" Robert replied. Ryan continued to chow down on his food.

Liam answered, "We are good to go. As soon as you get home, get ready to roll and we will pick you up at 3:30 sharp!"

His friends were all excited as they gave him high fives.

They continued with their day. When the final bell rang throughout the school, Liam ran to his locker and back over to Boo's side of the school. Boo was already at her locker gathering her things and putting on her coat. Even though she was young, she was already a diva. Her outfits always had to match, and she always wore some of her mom's old jewelry with a mixture of her charm bracelets. As Liam approached Boo she said, "What are you so happy about? You seem quite happy considering you're going back up to the lake house for the weekend."

Liam answered, "I like the lake house fine. It's just the last time I was up there – I"

Boo interrupted, "I know, I know you saw a werewolf, and you've been seeing it in your dreams ever since, blah, blah, blah. Stop trying to scare me. You know it isn't going to work."

Liam answered happily, "I'm happy because Ryan and Robert are coming up with us!"

Boo rolled her eyes and said, "Ryan is okay. He's like a big teddy bear. But Robert creeps me out. I wish he was staying home."

Liam laughed. "I know, Robert is a bit much at times. But basically he's harmless. Known him forever. I promise you he won't try to scare you. Hurry up, Boo. He have to start walking home. Dad is busy packing up the car right now."

As soon as they got home, they found their parents in the driveway playing Tetris with the luggage and the supplies. "Well, it wouldn't be a problem if Liam didn't invite his—" Will started to say.

Annie saw them and interrupted, "It's okay, hon. Hey, kids. How was school? Are you ready to go?"

Liam replied, "Just need a few minutes, Mom, and then we should be good to go."

Annie said with a smile, "Great. We need a few minutes to figure out storage. Meet us back out here when you're ready."

Within a few minutes, they were on their way to Ryan's and Robert's houses. They both had a bag each. Will was driving and Annie was riding shotgun. Annie rolled down the window and said, "Just hold on to your bags or put them below the seat, boys. We ran out of room."

Both Ryan and Robert hopped into the far back row of seats, and they were on their way up north. "Everybody good?" Will asked. "There will be a few pit stops along the way. Dinner is going to burgers and fries while we get fuel. After that, our final destination shall be Iron River, Michigan."

CHAPTER 19

....

AN ORANGE MOON IN THE SKY

They drove along the Green Bay Bridge by the time was sun was setting. The temperature was dropping fast as the winds picked up out of the west. The Green Bay Bridge was considered the halfway point for their journey up north. Robert kept himself busy by playing games on his tablet and listening to music on his headphones. Ryan started to grow anxious and wondered how long it would take for them to arrive. "How much longer do we have until we get there?" Ryan asked as he stared out of his window.

"Just halfway there, brother," Liam said with a smile.

Ryan answered, "The longest I ever been in the car was for a Bears–Packers game in Green Bay."

Liam replied, "We still have to go through several small towns before we reach the UP Michigan border. By the time we hit Crystal Falls, we will basically be there. Crystal Falls is the closest big town from Iron River. About fifteen miles east of the lake house."

"What are the sleeping arrangements?" Ryan asked.

Liam answered, "Well, my grandparents will have one bedroom, my parents will be in another. I'll be sleeping in the camper with you, Robert, and Boo. There are plenty of beds, and plus we will have our own space away from the parental units."

"A camper! That sounds pretty cool," Ryan replied.

"Yeah! You and Robert will sleep in the bunk beds in the back part of the camper, I will sleep in the bedroom, and Boo will sleep on the sofa bed. There's plenty of room, and the camper has a microwave and a TV. We can stay up late, make popcorn, and watch movies if we want."

"Sounds like a plan to me! Now I'm really excited. What else can we do while we are up there?" Ryan questioned.

"The family still has their boat in the water alongside the dock. We can go for a boat ride, kayak, hike, run, bike, and the lake even has a park on the other side that has a basketball court. We won't be able to do water games since the water temperature will be too cold. But at night we can make a campfire, make s'mores, and check out my dad's telescope. On clear nights you can basically see the whole Milky Way galaxy."

Ryan was satisfied with Liam's answers and continued to stare out of his window. "You're not kidding about the night sky, Liam. Take a look at that moon, man!" Ryan exclaimed. "I don't think I've seen a moon that orange before!"

"I believe that's almost considered the Halloween moon, Ryan," Will said.

"Is your dad a part-time astronomy teacher or something?" Robert asked.

Liam answered, "No. He's just really into science, especially biology, chemistry, and astronomy. Total nerd in school but he was one of the nerdy athletic kids."

Will continued, "Well, that's not considered the full moon yet. The full moon won't happen for a couple of days. Each day it will grow more full. It should help brighten the landscape for me. I don't like to drive up here after dark."

"Why is that, sir?" Ryan asked.

Will answered, "It gets really dark along these roads at night, boys. A lot of wilderness and a lot of wildlife are more active at that time. So keep your eyes peeled for me please."

When Liam saw the large orange moon rising over the tree line, he started to feel nervous. He thought, *Maybe Dad is right. Maybe it is my overactive imagination acting up again. What do I have to worry about? I'm surrounded by family and friends. I'm sure if there was a serious problem, my grandparents wouldn't allow us to visit. Just keep your cool. Especially around these guys. They're your friends, but they can spot weakness a mile away.*

Just after 10:00 p.m., they finally arrived at the lake house. The grandparents had arrived about an hour before them. Tina was already in bed. Daniel had made a fire near the edge of the property along the lake. He came up to greet them and help them unpack. "How was your trip up, Will?" Daniel said, shaking Will's hand.

"Long as per usual but not bad considering. No traffic after Green Bay. We made it up here in pretty good time." Will carried an assortment of bags from the van.

Daniel looked over to Liam and his friends and said, "This must be your friends, Liam. Nice to meet you. The camper is ready for you. Inside you'll find some snacks on the counter and some soda in the fridge. Had the heater on since we arrived. So it should be nice and warm in there. The temperature is going down into the 40s tonight."

They all said thank you as they got themselves situated for the night.

That night they settled in nicely inside the camper. They enjoyed the snacks and watched a movie together before they all decided it was time for bed. As Liam went into his bedroom and settled into bed, he couldn't help but think if he would hear anything outside the camper overnight. The bedroom had a small window that faced the next-door neighbor's house. Liam could hear some extra commotion from the neighbor's house and some voices he didn't recognize. The voices sounded like that of a younger people like himself. Liam figured maybe the next-door neighbor's grandkids came up to visit for the weekend. He settled in nicely knowing that his friends were just down the hall from where he was sleeping. Liam drifted off to sleep and happily didn't wake up until the following morning.

CHAPTER 20

....

MY FRIENDS MEET
THE NEIGHBORS

L iam awoke the next morning by the sounds of Ryan and Robert walking and talking outside the camper. They were exploring the property while Boo gave them the nickel tour. Liam walked outside and down the stairs and could smell the wonderful cooking from inside the main house. *Grandma and Dad must be cooking up a nice spread*, he thought, and continued to walk up the outside stairs and open the side door.

"Liam! There you are! Come here and give Grandma a kiss!" Tina welcomed him with a huge hug.

"What are you and Dad cooking, Grandma?" Liam questioned.

Will answered as he was getting biscuits out of the oven. "Made a nice firehouse breakfast spread. Eggs, bacon, and biscuits with gravy. Go tell everyone that the food is ready, Son."

They all sat down for their breakfast. All of them took a healthy portion of food, especially Ryan. Ryan went up for seconds or thirds. Liam wasn't sure since he lost count after a while. "Looks like the weather is going for sunny and warm today, boys," Will said. He finished his breakfast and coffee.

"Really? What's the temperature going to be today?"

Will answered, "Surprisingly in the high 70s today. Should be a great day to do almost everything, boys. I ask that you help with one thing before you begin your Northern Wilderness Adventure. Just help with the dishes."

They all agreed and then headed down to the dock to take a look around the lake.

Ryan, Robert, and Liam all walked down to the end of the dock. "Wow!" Robert exclaimed. "The water is so beautiful here. I don't think I've ever seen water so clear before. You can see right down to the bottom."

Ryan looked over toward the next-door neighbor's house. "Never mind the water, I know I've never seen her before."

They all looked over to see a beautiful girl sunbathing in a swimsuit.

"Liam! Who is that?" Ryan questioned.

"I'm not sure but she looks like she doesn't want to be bothered by any of us, lads. She looks like she's old enough to be in high school."

"Well, Liam, you're always the go-to guy when it comes to breaking the ice with the ladies. Why don't you introduce yourself. You can skip the introductions for Robert, but make sure you tell her I'm single," said Ryan.

"You know I can hear everything you little creeps are saying!" the young lady exclaimed, looking over to us.

"Say what?" Liam questioned with a slight stutter.

"Up here you can hear someone's personal conversations from across the lake. If you don't believe, try it," she said.

"Who are you?" Liam questioned.

"I'm Rita. I'm Larry and Gabby's granddaughter. And that slightly older one over there is my older brother, Mike."

Mike walked outside from the sliding glass door from the back of the house. Mike looked like he was in his late high school years. He was wearing gym shorts, a muscle shirt, and silver aviator shades. He was tall, athletic, and had spiked blonde hair. "These little jerks giving you trouble, sis?" Mike questioned as he stared at all of them.

"I'm not sure yet. If we were back home, I would say yes, so you could chase them away for me. But this must be some of the grandkids that Daniel and Tina were talking about. Since they're neighbors, I guess I'll be nice."

Liam replied, "Yes. Daniel and Tina are my grandparents. I'm Liam. My sister, Boo, is with my parents right now. And these are my friends Robert and Ryan."

Ryan looked at Mike and said, "Nice to meet you, bro. You look like you play some ball. What position do you play? Are you junior varsity?"

Mike replied, "First off I'm not your bro, little man. And yes I do play ball. I'm a junior, but I play on the varsity team. Starting linebacker. I would be playing a game this weekend but instead we got pulled up here."

"What do you mean?" Liam questioned, looking at Rita and Mike.

Rita replied, "You don't know what's going on?"

"No," Liam replied.

Mike and Rita both looked at each other and then looked back at them. Mike said, "Tell you what, why don't you give us a few minutes, we will all take a walk and I'll fill you in."

They agreed and waited for Rita and Mike near the front of their property. Within a few minutes, Rita changed into a summer outfit, and both Rita and Mike exited their house and walked toward them. Robert chimed up and said to Rita, "So Rita, if Mike is a junior, what year of high school are you?"

Rita answered, "I'm a freshman. It's a bit of an adjustment, but I have my big brother on campus with me. He is a huge help."

Mike looked at everyone and said, "Let's walk down this way, where there are fewer parents and adults around."

They walked down the road as a group, and Mike said, "So your parents, your grandparents, didn't fill you in on what happened to our grandpa?"

Liam exclaimed, "Who, Larry? What happened!"

Mike sighed. "He went on a hunting trip west of here along the wilderness. He hunts wild turkey this time of year." He paused as he got choked up but continued, "He never came back. The local and state police set up a grid search along the area where he camped. They found his truck, some camping gear, but not him. Not even his weapons. We are here with our mom to help our grandmom. Figure we can be here for moral support until something is known. Or at the very least help her pack up and head back to our house. Presently, my grandfather is considered a missing person."

Rita broke into the conversation and said, "But Mike and I have been doing some detective work of our own. We've been finding out a lot of weird stuff about this area. We've been doing some research at the local library."

"Why the local library?" Liam questioned.

"A lot of the history of the area is not published on the internet. We found out a lot of interesting facts about this town from old news reels and preserved newspapers. Yeah, we even ran into an old lady who lives on the lake here. She began talking to us after she heard of our grandpa's disappearance. She told us some stuff that we couldn't even find in the library. You see those purple plants that are along the edge of everyone's property?"

"Yeah," they all said. Mike continued, "Those are called wolf's-bane."

Ryan looked up at Mike and said, "What the hell is wolf's-bane!"

Robert said, "Wolf's-bane is a deterrent for werewolves!"

Liam's stomach began to turn.

Ryan exclaimed, "Wait! What? Werewolves? You mean like Svengoolie old-school-movie werewolves?"

"That's a possibility. We figured the most common explanation was a black bear attack. But if it was a bear attack, some remains of my grandfather would have been found. And this town has a long history of disappearances and people who went missing along the western wilderness and the Ottawa National Forest. I overheard my grandmother talking to one of my grandpa's old buddies from the state police on the phone. He told her that the claw marks at the campsite were much larger than anything they ever seen from any previous bear attack. And that old lady said that she's worried that the wolf's-bane will die soon from the cooler nights we've been having along the lake."

"What's happens when the wolf's-bane dies?" Liam asked.

"I'm not sure, but I think we need to try to do some more research at the library. If you're willing to help, just hop into my jeep. I'll drive."

They walked back to the house. Robert said, "So, there was reason why you freaked out at my house. You saw a legit werewolf up here didn't you?"

Liam replied questionably, "Maybe... I don't know. But things are starting to add up, and now I'm getting nervous. Maybe it's best if I talk to my folks."

"Are you kidding me? This may be my only chance to actually be a part of a werewolf mystery. Don't screw this up for me!" Robert said.

Liam's jaw clenched. "I'm less worried about you living out one of your horror movies and more worried about our safety right now."

Ryan got in between his friends and said, "Guys! Calm down! Now you both heard what Mike said. The adults around here, including the real adults like police, were completely unable to help his family. What's it gonna hurt if we help them out a little bit."

Robert chimed in with condescending tone. "You just want to help out Rita since you have an instant dream weaver crush on her!"

Ryan replied, "Maybe you're right. Rita sure is a smoke show. But let's just try to help them and see where it leads us."

"What should I say to my parents?" Liam questioned.

Ryan said, "Just keep it cool. Just say we are going to town to get ice cream with our new friends from next door. I'm sure your parents won't question too much."

The gamble worked. Liam went up to his mom, since his dad and Boo just set up along the lakefront to fish. Even though he didn't catch anything all season, Will was persistent and Boo usually had better luck. Annie came outside to introduce herself to Mike and Rita. "Thanks for taking these boys into town. Try to have them home by dinner please. Here's some money; go have fun and be safe."

"Thanks, Mom, will do," Liam said. Liam ran over to Mike's jeep and hopped into the back seat with Ryan and Robert. Next stop was the Iron River Public Library.

CHAPTER 21

....

THE PURSUIT OF INFORMATION

The ride into town was a short one. Within a few minutes of driving along Sunset Valley Lake Road, they passed up the old mansion where Liam once saw the strange old man. There was no movement in and around the property from where he could see. They then passed up the road that led to the picnic beach area of the lake, and they quickly approached Route 2. On their way to the Iron River Public Library, they drove past the town ice cream stand. It would have been a good idea to go there, but it wasn't open for a couple of hours.

The Iron River Public Library was one street over from the town's main street. Located within the center of the town, the library shared a parking area with the town hall and police department. Across the street from the library was St. Agnes Church. It was a beautiful old Catholic church. Liam always appreciated such things since he was an altar server back home for St. Constance Parish. Outside the church were beautiful religious statues and a large silver cross over the main entrance. During the summer and vacation weekends, St. Agnes Church was the family's church away from home. Mike parked his car in the parking lot, and they all hopped out almost in unison. As Mike exited his jeep, he looked back at St. Agnes Church and noticed an older woman walking into the main entrance. He turned and looked at Rita and said, "Hey, sis. Check it out. Isn't that the old lady we talked to about the wolf's-bane and such?"

Rita looked across the street toward the old woman. The old woman took notice of the group looking in their general direction.

Before walking into the building she paused, smiled, and waved at them as they waved back. Rita said, "Yup. It's definitely her. If I remember correctly, she is a retired nurse but volunteers at the church and at the senior center in Crystal Falls."

Mike replied, "I'm sure she could help answer a few more questions we have about the area. But let's see what else we can find out at the library first."

They all walked through the outside courtyard of the library. It was a beautiful place where they held elementary summer programs for younger kids. The program's success was partly thanks to Annie who helped come up with great educational ideas. They had plenty of activities for the preschool and kindergarten age groups and even promoted their summer evening movie nights where families could watch movies in their outside movie theater. Robert saw the advertisement for the upcoming movies. One of which was going to be played later that evening.

"Hey, guys, check it out! They're playing one of my favorite kid Halloween movies tonight. You think maybe we can check it out?" Robert asked.

Ryan looked down at Robert and said, "Aren't you a little old for that kid stuff, dude? Plus, we don't know where this investigation is going to lead us, so let's focus of that."

Robert replied, "Sure thing, Romeo. Maybe Rita has a thing for young dudes who are nowhere near the driving age."

Liam got in between Robert and Ryan and said, "Guys. Look. Ryan is somewhat right. Right now, let's try to find out what we can. Maybe it will help Mike and Rita figure out what happened to their grandpa. Maybe at the very least it will bring the family closure."

Robert replied, "What's in it for you, Liam?"

Liam answered, "Maybe it will bring some closure for me too. I haven't been able to get that image out of my mind since.... since—"

Ryan interrupted, "Since what, dude?"

Liam replied, "Never mind. Let's just help them out and see where it leads us. Deal?"

Both Ryan and Robert turned to Liam and said, "Deal!"

As they walked into the main entrance, Liam noticed several memorable plaques signifying substantial monetary contributions from the Schubert family. He looked at one of the pictures that portrayed the classic ribbon-cutting ceremony for the library. Liam took notice that the old man from the mansion was the one with the big scissors. He could only assume that was old Mr. Schubert. He was standing next to what looked like local politicians and the chief of police. In the picture Liam recognized a younger Nick Rosalie holding his son and several other town residents. The library also had several pieces of artwork signifying the local native Menominee and Ojibwe tribes. It was basically a small gallery that paid tribute to one of the native chiefs who painted all kinds of pictures, including the painting that Mr. Rosalie had in his shop. The paintings along with a few Native American artifacts were displayed behind glass. Over the display, a memorable plaque read: "In Honor of Chief Big Bear Toe. Thank you for your Honor, Leadership and Bravery."

Liam followed the main hallway into a branch corridor. To the right was the children's books section. To the left was the traditional fiction and nonfiction sections, including the history section. In the back of the history section there was a room with a sign along the threshold that read: "Discover the History of Iron River." That's where Liam found the group. Mike and Rita were looking through old newspapers that were put into a digital format on the library database. Ryan was looking over Rita's shoulder and trying to help her, of course. Robert was actually fascinated by some of the books that told the history of the local area. Robert was looking through a book that was more like an old encyclopedia textbook that gave the history of the Menominee and Ojibwe tribes.

As Robert examined some of the pages, he said, "Hey, guys. Check this out."

They walked over to Robert to find out what he discovered. Liam said, "What did you find out, dude?"

Robert answered, "It says here that the Menominee and Ojibwe tribes have lived in this area for hundreds of years. They live mostly on the whatever the land provides. They are talented farmers and hunters. Says here that back in the 70s, Chief Big Bear Toe went through legal negotiations with the local government to hold title over his descendants farming and hunting lands, which stretch from the western coast of UP Michigan to the western boundaries of the Ottawa National Forest. To this day, the area west of the Ottawa

National Forest to the coast is considered a Native American Reserve and preserved as a wilderness region where only a select number of outside hunters can hunt only at the direction of the local tribes. You said your grandpa was in this area when he went missing, correct?"

After Robert read the information to them they all looked at each other.

Mike said, "So maybe if the state and local police are unable to help maybe, we can talk to the local tribes out there. Rita was able to find an old map of the area in the archives. What did you find, Sis?"

Rita went over to the computer screen and hit the print icon of an old map. Rita said, "This is what I found. The legal negotiations with the local government and the native tribes had to draw up legal boundary lines of the territory in order to complete the deal. This map shows where the tribes hold claim over the land, and it also shows how to access their main gathering and various campsites, which change given the seasons."

Ryan looked up at both Liam and Robert and said, "She's beautiful *and* smart, boys. A man could only be so lucky."

They rolled their eyes as they looked over at Mike who was growing tired of Ryan flirting with his sister. Mike chimed in, "I think I found one more thing. Check this out!"

Mike had accessed the PDF files of old local newspapers. "I searched for hunting accidents in the database. Found this and it's pretty interesting. It says here that back in the day that old man Mr. Schubert's brother died in the horrific hunting accident somewhere west of the Ottawa National Forest. All signs lead to a bear attack, but the county coroner stated that man died from substantially large animal bites and claw wounds. It also says that Mr. Schubert and a few local hunters were together during this hunting trip. The article mentions the names Nick Rosalie and Rich Patterson."

Astonished by the news, Liam said, "Nick Rosalie is the man who owns that antique shop in town. My dad is friends with this local Iron River cop named Bobby. His dad is Nick Rosalie, and I believe my dad said that Bobby's boss is Chief Patterson. This is all hitting way too close to home, guys. What do we do next?"

CHAPTER 22

....

FIRST STOP PIZZA, NEXT STOP THE WILDERNESS

Mike looked up at each of them and then looked down at his watch. "It's still early enough in the afternoon. Anyone else getting hungry? I suggest getting something to eat, and we all take a drive out to the wilderness area ourselves. I'll drive, of course."

Ryan questioned, "What's good to eat in this little town? I saw the typical fast-food places, but we've been eating that stuff since we left home. Any suggestions?"

Liam answered Ryan saying, "My family and I have eaten at that pizza place just down the road on Main Street. It's called Rosalie's Pizza. I believe Nick Rosalie and his wife own and operate it."

Mike seemed happy with the suggestion. "Sounds like a plan. Everyone good with that choice?"

Everyone looked at each other and shrugged. They gathered all the information they printed and headed out to Mike's jeep. Within minutes, they were parked in front of Rosalie's Pizza. The time that they arrived was perfect. It was too late for the lunch crowd and too early for the dinner crowd. The hostess sat them right away, and next they were greeted by one of the owners, Meg Rosalie. "How you doing, young people? First time here? Now, I recognize one of you. You're Liam, aren't you? Your dad is friends with my son, Bobby."

Liam answered, "Yes, ma'am, that is correct. These are friends from out of town. Figure I'll show them around town and get something to eat while we are out."

Meg questioned, "Now, do you need time to look at the menu or do you know what you would like?"

Liam said, "We'll just do one of the extra-large cheese and pepperoni pizzas please and sodas for each."

Of course Ryan chimed up and said, "And an order of the breadsticks, dipping sauce, and a basket of cheese fries please."

Liam rolled my eyes as he reached into his pocket to count the money his mother gave him before they left the house. Ryan looked at Liam and said, "Don't worry, bro. I got you. My parents gave me some spending money before we left Chicago." Ryan looked over to Rita and said with a wink, "In fact, I have enough cash for a few dinners out and maybe a trip to the movies if this town even has one."

Mike took a deep breath out of frustration and said, "Now, Liam, you said that lady's husband is Nick Rosalie?"

Liam answered, "Yes."

Mike replied, "Let's not mention anything to her about what we are doing until we try to investigate ourselves. She seemed like the type that has a mind like a steel trap. She remembered you perfectly as soon as you walked into the door." Mike looked out at the printouts and continued, "These printouts will be good for us. As we get further into the Ottawa Forest, we will probably lose our cell phone signal. From my current GPS, it looks like not a far drive from here. Less than an hour. We continue to head west on Route 2 through the forest and the road branches off further when you reach the wilderness."

Meg walked over with the breadsticks, french fries, and drinks. Mike covered up the printouts under his jacket in the booth. As she was within a few feet of their table, Mike and rest of the group grew quiet. "So what's on the agenda for the rest of the day for you young adults?" Meg questioned.

They all looked at each other and Robert chimed in, "Maybe check out that skateboard park you have and play some softball on the diamond nearby. Afterward we were thinking of getting ice cream at the stand and maybe checking out the movie playing at the library tonight."

With a smile Meg said, "Well, that sounds like a full day but a fun one for sure. Let me know if you need anything. Your pizza should be up shortly."

As she walked away, Mike continued, "Yeah it looks like just under an hour drive from here until we reach the wilderness section. As soon as we are done here, we will head straight out that way. I suggest texting your parents, Liam, and say you're hanging out with us for dinner tonight. You don't know how long we will be without a cell phone connection. Rita, text Mom as well. That way she doesn't worry about us either. If she starts asking a lot of questions, just give her that phony story that Robert gave that old lady."

Liam did as Mike suggested and then asked, "How long do you think we will be out there? And are we going to try to find the native tribes?"

Mike answered, "I'm not sure right now to be honest. I'm just going to figure it out as we go. But I want to be home by the early evening just to avoid suspicion."

Everyone was enjoying the snacks before the main course, especially Ryan. He took out almost a whole basket of cheese fries by himself. Meg approached with the pizza, put one of those center racks in the middle of the table, and handed each of them new plates, setting Parmesan cheese and sweet pepper spice on the table. Meg smiled and said, "I'll refill those drinks for you, enjoy."

Mike answered, "Thank you, ma'am. And can you please get the check ready too? Hand it over to my friend Ryan here. He's the one with the deep pockets."

Ryan looked up from his half-eaten slice of pie at Mike with a curious look on his face. "What the hell, man?"

Mike exclaimed, "You have a problem with that! Keep hitting on my sister and I'll make you fill up my gas tank too."

Ryan immediately backed off and said, "Okay…okay sorry."

Rita rolled her eyes, winked at Ryan, and said with a smile, "He's my big brother. He's a bit of the protective type."

Within a few moments, they were finished with their meal. Ryan paid the check and they were all on their way out the door toward Mike's jeep. Meg thanked the group for coming and bagged up some extra fries for Ryan since he liked them so much. Meg waved goodbye from the front counter and said, "Have fun and be safe out there." Little did she know that soon they would be nowhere near safety.

CHAPTER 23

....

THE WILDERNESS

They headed west along Route 2 just as the GPS suggested. The forest was beautiful especially with the colors of fall along the endless row of trees. The leaves were falling steadily along the road and into the forest. The colors were brilliant, ranging from yellow to orange to red and brown. The weather added to the day's beauty by producing crystal clear blue skies with the temperature in the low 70s. As Mike drove along, he turned to Rita who was riding shotgun and said, "We passed Watersmeet a while ago. How much longer until we reach the wilderness, Sis?"

Rita looked at her phone and said, "I checked my phone a couple of minutes ago. It said just a few miles longer, but now I'm not getting a signal."

Mike looked back at Rita and said, "Figured as much. Best to look at the map printouts for the rest of the trip. Should be there soon."

As they approached the end of Route 2, they noticed that the road became smaller and branched off in different directions. Mike slowed down his jeep to look at the brown sign along the road which said, "Welcome to the Porcupine Mountains Wilderness." Underneath that sign it read, "Left to Lake Gogebic, Right to Native Reservation Area (Public Access Restricted)." Mike looked at this sister and back at the group and said, "Well gang, what do you think we should do? Go left or go right?"

Everyone was silent as they looked at each other.

Liam answered, "This is your grandpa, Mike. What do you want to do?"

Mike replied, "Well, I heard my grandmother mention something about Lake Gogebic to my mom. Something about my grandfather's campsite. Let's go left and at the very least see what we can find."

He drove the jeep to the left and along the narrow one-lane road further into the wilderness toward Lake Gogebic. Everyone was silent. Liam was sure that everyone felt a little uneasy. They were now far away from their grown-ups and far from any help that they could find. They drove along the road for several miles until they saw another brown sign stating, "Lake Gogebic Ahead." As they approached Lake Gogebic, Liam couldn't help to feel peaceful around the area. The lake was a long narrow lake that was supposed to be great for fishing. They parked close to the water's edge and exited the jeep.

The water was perfectly clear, even more so than back at the lake house. From the water's edge Liam could see right down to the bottom of the water. From there he could see various families of fish ranging from walleye, large-mouth bass, to northern pike. He couldn't help but think, *Even my dad could catch a fish or two in this lake*.

"What's the plan, Mike?" Ryan questioned as he looked around the area.

Mike took a few moments to gather his thoughts and come up with a strategy. Liam could tell Mike was a naturally born leader and people often relied on him for a plan of action. Mike said, "I figure it's best that we stick together, especially since we have no cell phone signal. The sun will start setting within a few hours. I suggested going this way since the ground looks well-traveled. Maybe that's where the police headed during their search. I believe most of Grandpa's belongings including his truck were taken to some state police facility for chain of custody and evidence. But that doesn't mean we can't find something."

The group liked that idea, especially Liam. He didn't want to branch off from the main group. He was already nervous, and splitting up would have made it worst. They set course toward the trail made from previous visitors. What struck Liam the most was how incredibly quiet the area was. No sirens, cars, air travel, or loud music. Just the sound of nature and the group. Mike was on point.

Liam shouted up to Mike and said, "Hey, Mike. What if some of the bigger wilderness creatures find us? What do we do then?"

Mike turned around, smiled, and said, "Well, if we hear or see anything we can't handle, then it's time to hightail it out of here and straight back to my jeep."

They searched around for over an hour and didn't find anything. They were growing tired, and Liam was growing more anxious as they got farther away from the vehicle. They soon found an old road. The group followed the old road down to where it was chained and locked. Around the fence there were several signs reading: "No Trespassing Beyond This Point, Hazardous Area, Abandoned Mine Shafts." Liam turned to Mike and said, "What do you make of this, Mike?"

Mike answered, "Like the sign says. It's some of the old mines that closed down years ago. The security lock looks new, which is odd, but it hasn't been tampered with. So we know my grandpa hasn't been here."

Rita was growing much more tired after a long journey of finding nothing. Liam was appreciative of Rita suggesting, "Hey, Mike. Let's start turning around. Maybe on the way back we can check that one patch of open area along the woods. If there's nothing, it's probably best if we pack this up for the day."

Mike thought about it for a minute, looked up toward the setting sun along the horizon, and said, "Yeah you're right; let's do that. Damn it. Feel like we came all the way here for nothing!"

Rita gave her brother a hug, since she could sense his frustration, and said, "At least we made it this far. We can always come back and hopefully talk to the natives."

The group headed back toward the vehicle until they reached the open area that Rita mentioned. They walked along the area until Robert spotted something ahead. "Hey, guys, check this out!" They ran over to him.

Liam said to Robert, "What did you find, dude?"

Robert bent down and picked up a long piece of yellow police tape, which read: "Michigan State Police Line Do Not Cross." Robert gave it to Mike, and they all walked farther through a patch of rough trail until they noticed another clear area near a small river branch that streamed from Lake Gogebic. Mike looked around and noticed some more police tape. Mike looked at everyone and said, "This must be the place where Grandpa set up camp. We found it!" he exclaimed. "Spread out around this area. See if you can find anything."

The group did as Mike directed them to do. They were a few minutes away from the jeep, but it was now approaching dusk. Mike suggested they use the flashlights on their phones since they were losing the daylight. When Liam turned on his flashlight, he noticed something shining along the water's edge. He approached the object and picked it up. It was a bullet shell casing! Being excited over his discovery, Liam shouted over to Mike, "Mike! Look what I found."

Mike and the rest of the crew ran over to Liam. Mike took a look at the shell casing and examined it. He exclaimed, "This is from my grandfather's hunting rifle for sure! I went on a few hunts with him closer to home. He wouldn't have taken a shot in camp without something coming into camp being a threat! Good job, Liam!"

Ryan shined his light at a nearby tree and said, "Hey, guys! Are those claw marks on this tree?"

Mike shined his light on the tree. "Holy crap! Look at the size of these claw marks! This looks like something a lot bigger than your typical gray wolf or even a bear." Mike looked at the claw marks with his light for another few seconds and said, "Let's get out of here right now!"

They all liked that suggestion, given the evidence at the campsite and now the sun had set over the trees. The moon was now rising. The group ran back to the jeep within a few minutes. They were glad to make it back for the trip home. They each took a minute to catch their breath, especially Robert. Ryan looked at Robert and said, "Damn, dude, don't you ever exercise?"

Robert was still catching his breath. "Yeah, bro. When I'm playing baseball with you idiots. And gym class too. That's enough cardio for me." They all giggled over Robert's and Ryan's interaction, and then they froze where they stood. They heard a loud howl. It sounded close by.

Ryan turned to Mike and said, "What the hell was that, Mike?"

Mike took a big gulp as he got his car keys out of his pocket and exclaimed, "I don't know, and I don't what to know. All I know is it sounds big and not far away. Everyone in the jeep! We are leaving!"

CHAPTER 24

....

THE RIDE HOME

"Mike! Make a U-turn and let's get out of here!" Rita exclaimed as she hopped into the shotgun position of the jeep.

"That's the plan, Sis!" Mike quickly turned the vehicle around, put it into drive, and headed back toward Route 2.

As they drove out of the area Liam turned around. He could only hear the sound of the vehicle's engine and the screech of the tires along the path. Liam no longer heard the sounds of nature. The little critters in the wilderness fell silent as though hiding from a predator. He turned around to see tree branches and bushes move quickly from one side to the other. It was hard to make out what he was seeing, giving that fact that they were surrounded by dusky wilderness and almost complete darkness. But then there was no question! Liam saw the beast and the pair of yellow eyes that haunted him, his memories, and his dreams since that horrible night. The same chill went down his spine, his jaw dropped, and Liam became frozen in fear. He was sitting in the middle in between Ryan and Robert. They both noticed his reaction. Ryan asked Liam, "What is it, dude?"

Both Ryan and Robert turned around and saw the beast charging toward them! Robert and Ryan's jaws dropped as well. They both looked at each other. Robert said, "Okay, this is too real now. I don't like this! I'm ready to go back home and never watch another horror movie again! Mike, step on the gas, bro!"

Mike looked into the rearview mirror and saw the evil yellow eyes in the near distance and the beast charging toward his car!

Rita also looked through the side mirror and let out a high-pitched scream!

Mike exclaimed, "Holy crap! What the hell is that thing?! Hold on!" Mike put his foot on the accelerator all of the way down to the floor. The jeep charged through the narrow road without a problem. The beast was still chasing them, but the distance between it and the jeep grew longer. Just ahead they saw a sign reading: "Thank You for Visiting The Porcupine Mountains Wilderness." Ryan saw the sign and said, "Yeah no thanks, I think I'll pass on coming here again!" After they passed up that sign, the next sign just down the road stated: "Route 2 Ahead."

As they sped along Route 2, Liam looked back to check out the road and if the beast was still chasing them. To his relief, Liam no longer saw the beast! He thought, *It must have given up after a while. We should be safe.* Liam tapped Mike on the shoulder with a sign of relief in his voice saying, "Mike, I think we are good. I don't see it anymore. We lost it!"

Mike nodded his head and said, "Thanks but I'd rather be sure. I'm going to keep this up until we are reach Iron River. First stop is straight to the police station in town."

They continued to go at a high rate of speed along Route 2. They quickly approached Watersmeet. Mike said to Rita, "Sis, you should have cell phone signal now. Check to see if you have any messages."

Rita looked at her phone and said, "Nothing. Just a few text messages from friends back home."

Liam looked at his phone. He, too, had cell phone signal now. He had a voice mail from his mother. Liam listened the message which stated, "Hey, sweetie. It's Mom. Boo wants to know if you can pick her up some ice cream on your way home. She wants a banana split. And one for Grandpa as well. Let me know when you get this please. Love you, bye." Liam was about to call his mother back when he noticed a state police squad car waiting just along the road on the outstretch of town. He could see that the officer had his radar gun out and pointed it toward their direction.

Liam tapped Mike on the shoulder and said, "Mike! Slow down, dude. The cops are going to pull us over if you don't!"

Mike looked into the rearview mirror only to see the police car come to life with lights and sirens and drive quickly in their direction. Rita grew nervous as Mike refused to pull over. They were now in a high-speed police pursuit. Rita exclaimed, "Mike! For God's sake pull over the car! He doesn't know what happened. Maybe he can help us!"

Mike started to yell at Rita saying, "Rita! Please just be quiet. I'm going to keep driving until we get to Iron River. It's just a few miles ahead. I'll explain our situation when we get there. Right now I want to be in a town with light and more help on hand."

✦ ✦ ✦

Meanwhile, back in Iron River, Chief Patterson was in his office when he heard the commotion on the scanner. This particular evening Bobby and Sergeant Pat Fitzgerald were the only two officers on duty. Chief Patterson opened his office door and walked to the front desk. Bobby was sitting there waiting for his sergeant to return. Chief Patterson asked, "Hey, Bobby. Where's Pat? Do you hear what going on over the radio?"

Bobby answered, "To answer your question, Chief, the sarge wanted me to wait here at the front desk while he went out to the coffee shop to pick up some joe and pastries. And no, I haven't heard anything. Something going on, Chief?"

The chief rolled his eyes and said, "Bobby, check the volume of the scanner. Pat probably turned it down so he could read his book."

Bobby looked at the scanner and said, "You're right, Chief! Sarge must have turned the volume down. Sorry for not noticing."

Chief replied, "Never mind that, Bobby! Just listen. Sounds like there's a high-speed pursuit heading into our area."

Bobby listened to the scanner which stated, "MSP (Michigan State Police) 145 to Iron River PD, MSP 145 to Iron River do you copy?"

The chief grabbed the hook from the scanner and replied, "MSP 145 this is Iron River. What's your message?"

The state trooper replied, "Iron River I'm in a high-speed pursuit of a group of kids in a jeep heading eastbound along Route 2. Requesting assistance and possible roadblock before they enter your town. ETA 3 minutes."

The chief replied, "Message received MSP 145. Sending two units your direction. We will be set up a roadblock just west of town."

"Bobby, get into your squad car now. I'll hold down the fort here. Meet up with Pat and set up that roadblock. Did Pat ever acknowledge the transmission?" Chief Patterson asked.

Bobby turned to the chief as he was running out the door and said, "He probably left his radio in the squad car. I'll drive down there and tell him myself." Bobby quickly got into his squad car, which was already facing out toward the street. He fired up the lights and sirens and quickly drove down Main Street toward the coffee shop. As he approached the coffee shop, Sergeant Fitzgerald was just exiting the shop with his container filled with coffee and another large bag filled with pastries. One of the pastries was hanging from the sergeant's mouth.

"Sarge!" Bobby shouted. "Where's your radio? We've been trying to reach you!"

Pat replied, "It's in my squad car next to my lottery tickets. Why? What's up?"

Bobby replied, "There's a high-speed pursuit coming into town with the state police that should be here any minute!"

Sarge threw the items into the back in his squad car and said, "Wait for me, kid. I got lead. Just follow and set up behind me!"

Both Bobby and Sarge were now on their way quickly down Main Street and onto Route 2. Sarge was in front blocking both lanes. Bobby followed his sergeant's orders and staged his squad car behind. Sergeant Fitzgerald grabbed his radio and said, "Iron River car 2 to Command."

Chief Patterson replied, "Go ahead Iron River car 2."

Pat answered, "Command, me and Bobby are in place waiting to intercept the vehicle and MSP."

Chief Patterson called for the Michigan State Police, "MSP 145 did you hear that message?"

The state trooper replied, "Message received Iron River Command. ETA to intercept one minute."

CHAPTER 25

....

A TOWN UNDER SEIGE

Bobby and Pat both waited as they saw the jeep and state trooper approaching quickly from the west. Bobby heard a car pull up behind him. Bobby figured it was the chief, but it was his father! "Bobby! What the hell is going on around here? I heard all of commotion from down at Mom's restaurant," Nick said as he approached his son.

"Dad, get out of here! It's not safe! There's a high-speed chase approaching!"

Nick took his son's advice and moved his car and walked over to the sidewalk.

"Dad!" Bobby said as he continued to shout at his father, "Dad, get inside somewhere. It's not safe."

Nick shouted back, "Kid! Who the hell do you think you're talking to? I can handle myself. Just focus on what you have to do!"

The group approached Iron River as fast as they could. They could now see the lights from the town's Main Street. It was a sign of relief given the circumstances. Then they saw the flashing lights from the two Iron River squad cars blocking the street ahead.

Rita shouted at Mike, "Mike! Stop the car! Please, Mike, stop the car! We made it back!"

Mike looked back at his sister and then took his foot off of the accelerator. He was within a few hundred feet of the Iron River roadblock. As he approached, Mike slowed down the vehicle even more. He came to a complete stop, put the car in park, and put his hands up into the air. The group all followed suit. The state trooper was now parked blocking the street behind us. There was nothing but complete darkness behind the state trooper vehicle. Pat grabbed his car radio mic, turned on the microphone, and said, "Turn off your vehicle, step out of the car with your hands up, and lay on the pavement!"

The group was all so scared. Not so much of being in trouble with the police but more from the events of the evening. They all followed the commands of the police as the cops approached them. The state trooper approached from behind, and the sergeant approached from the front, both with their guns drawn. Sarge looked at the group and said, "Wow! You're just a bunch of stupid kids." Sarge put his gun back into his holster, and he continued to talk to us. "Stand up, all of you! What the hell is the big idea? Doesn't your generation know you have to pull over when a cop commands you to do so? Someone better explain very fast!"

Chief Patterson broke into the radio asking, "Iron River Command to car 2. Update me on your situation please."

Sarge pressed the button on his radio and said, "Yeah, Chief, this is car 2. All we have are a bunch of kids in a jeep. Don't know much yet, but we will update you as such."

"Message received," the chief replied.

Bobby approached from the rear. Pat gave Bobby a hand signal to stay at his vehicle. Sarge looked at the state trooper and asked, "Where did you catch these idiots?"

The state trooper answered, "I clocked them going over 90 mph just east of Watersmeet. Been chasing them since."

Sarge shook his head. "You can put your arms down. Someone explain to me why you didn't pull over miles ago. Let's start with the race car driver. You look like the oldest one in the group."

They were all quiet to let Mike try his best to diffuse and explain the situation. Mike said, "Yes, sir. My name is Mike. My grandfather was the retired state trooper who went missing in the wilderness. We figured we would go there ourselves and try to find out some things. But we...um....we saw....saw something, sir, that we couldn't explain. Well, sir, it was enough for us to be more afraid of it than a high-speed police pursuit."

Sarge and the state trooper looked at each other in disbelief. Nick approached Bobby who was still waiting by his squad car.

Nick said, "I overheard some of what that kid was saying. Did he say he saw something out in the wilderness? I recognize the young lad there. Liam. That's your buddy's kid."

Just down the road was the library where several families were gathered to watch an outdoor movie. Because of the commotion and disturbance, several of them became onlooking bystanders. Sarge looked at Mike and said, "What the hell are you talking about? What exactly did you see, son?"

Mike looked frightened and puzzled and said, "It was a beast, sir. A big hairy scary beast with yellow—"

Just then there was loud howl that came from behind the state trooper's squad car. Somewhere in the pitch blackness. Both the state trooper and the sergeant turned directly toward the sound with flashlights and guns drawn. They moved forward since it was hard to see past the flashing LED lights of their vehicles. "What the hell was that?" Sarge exclaimed as he and the state trooper continued to move forward.

Nick Rosalie grabbed his son's shoulder. Bobby turned around and said, "What is it, Dad?"

Nick replied, "It's here, Son. I'll get the kids to the church. I'll explain later. Watch your six. Everyone run! Get out of here now!"

Just then there was a loud growl and quick movement coming out of the darkness, followed by a terrible cry for help as the state trooper was grabbed by the beast and taken back into the darkness!

Sarge stood there in disbelief, unable to assess what just happened. Through the darkness the group could see a few small bursts of fire coming from the trooper's weapon and high-pitched screaming. Sarge took cover behind the squad car. Bobby approached the Sarge from the rear. Sarge turned to Bobby and said, "Kid, I'm good here. Do what your father said. Get these kids out of here!"

Bobby shouted, "All of you, follow my dad. He will get you somewhere safe. Move! Go!"

The group all ran toward Mr. Rosalie, and they ran together toward the church. As they were running down the street, the onlookers and their families started to follow suit and ran in the same direction. Another Iron River squad car rolled down Main Street and parked right in front of Mr. Rosalie and the group. It was

Chief Patterson. Nick looked at the chief and said, "Rich, it's here! You got one officer down! I'm getting these kids to the church!"

Rich acknowledged Nick's statement and said, "Do it! I'll get these people and their families out of here!" The chief got on his intercom and shouted on the speaker, "By order of the chief of police, everyone go home immediately! Shelter in place until instructed otherwise!"

The sarge heard the orders echo through the night's sky as he continued to sweep the area and assess the scene. The screaming was gone now. Only a trail of blood and a couple shell casings littered the town street. Pat heard movement to his left, he turned with his weapon at the ready, and fired! He hit nothing but a tree. He heard a slight growl come from right behind him. He could smell the horrible stench coming off of the creature's body. He turned to return fire! Before he could do so, the beast swung his claws at his neck. Blood came rushing out of the sarge's neck as he was hurled to the ground. The last thing he saw was the yellow eyes and big sharp teeth coming toward his face. A high-pitched scream was heard from across Main Street, which was suddenly silenced.

The group ran with Mr. Rosalie as fast as they could. They got to the stairs of St. Agnes Church where the old lady from the neighborhood was waiting for the group to enter. With her silver cross around her neck, she held the door open for them saying, "Get in here now. The beast will not enter here. You'll be safe!"

Nick looked at the old lady and said, "It's come back! We'll finish it this time!"

She closed the door, and the group all ran into the church pews.

Bobby helped with the evacuation of all the families from the library. As the cars and trucks quickly headed east along Route 2, Bobby and Chief Patterson stood in the middle of the street facing westbound with their guns drawn protecting their people's egress. Bobby wanted to advance closer toward Sarge's squad car. Chief Patterson said, "Bobby, wait! Put your standard issue away, son. You'll need something with some extra kick. Come to back of my car." Chief Patterson opened his trunk. Inside were several long rifles fully loaded.

Bobby grabbed one of the weapons and said, "The long rifles are a good idea, Chief, with that bear out there."

Chief Patterson grabbed his long rifle and said, "That's not a bear, kid. And those aren't regular rounds in that magazine. Those are silver bullet rounds. Here's a couple extra magazines. It's a werewolf, Bobby! And you and me have to protect this town. Follow me!"

CHAPTER 26

....

NEED ASSISTANCE NOW!

Bobby and Chief Patterson continued to move closer toward the two empty squad cars. Nothing was heard now. The streets were deserted, and there was no movement past the squad cars. Bobby shouted out, "Sarge! Michigan 145! Anyone!" There was no reply.

The chief opened his radio on the Michigan State Police frequency. The chief said, "Iron River Police Command to Michigan State Police!"

After a few seconds, a voice echoed through the radio. "This is Michigan State Police, go ahead Iron River Command."

The chief replied, "MSP Emergency, emergency, emergency! We have possibly two officers down due to an animal attack! One Iron River PD and one state trooper. Send a complete emergency police response to our area immediately! Send two ambulances as well. We will secure the scene and attempt to assess the injured members!"

After a few more seconds, the voice from dispatch said, "Animal attack! What kind of animal, Command!"

The chief kept his composure and said, "We were unable to see what type of animal due to the conditions, but please send as much help as you can spare!"

Dispatch replied, "Message received Iron River Command. We will have state troopers on their way. We will also request assistance from Crystal Falls PD and two ambulances from the local hospital. All resources will be en route."

The chief replied, "Message received. We will be here waiting."

Bobby and the chief continued to move forward with their weapons and lights drawn at the ready. They moved past the squad cars. They squinted their eyes in order to see past the emergency lights and into the darkness. They moved past the squad cars and beamed their lights in order to pierce through the darkness of the night. As they moved their lights left and right, they were able to assess the carnage. There were trails of blood and bullet casings scattered along the street. They followed the blood trails and continued to press forward from the road to the ditch and into the forest. Bobby and the chief walked side by side with just a few feet in between them.

Bobby looked at the chief and said, "Chief, if we get out of this, you're going to have to explain all of this to me! Just what the hell are we dealing with? What do you mean a werewolf?"

The chief looked at Bobby as he continued to walk slightly past him and said, "Don't worry, kid. They'll be plenty of time to explain everything. Right now let's try to find our brothers!"

They continued to search along the grounds of the woods for several minutes. They followed the trail of blood left from the initial scene. They found blood on the ground, on the leaves, and brushed along the tree bark. Bobby pointed his weapon and light toward something lying on the ground just a few feet ahead of him. Bobby found something, but it was hard to tell what it was. Bobby looked toward the chief and said, "Chief! Over here! Found something!"

The chief looked at Bobby and pointed his light in the same direction. They moved forward toward the remains. Bobby followed behind the chief by a few feet. The chief was directly above the remains and said, "Oh my God! Oh no! No! Bobby just stay there please! Cover my six!"

Bobby did as the chief ordered and said, "What is it, Chief? Is it…?"

The chief put on some gloves he had in his pocket and kneeled alongside the bodies. "Yeah, Bobby, it's them. I'll assess them. Just stay there!" The chief assessed both the state trooper and Sergeant Fitzgerald.

Bobby replied, "Chief, I'll go back to my squad car and pick up my medical gear from my trunk. I have that emergency trauma care kit."

The chief turned to Bobby and said, "Son, just stay here with me. There's no need for that gear. Both of these men are gone. They've been chewed up and lost too much blood. They aren't breathing, and they don't have a pulse. They're gone." The chief looked down at the two fallen officers for a few minutes. Bobby moved closer in disbelief of what the chief said to him. Bobby took one look at the bloody carnage and vomited behind a tree. The chief pressed his talk button on his radio. "Iron River Command to Michigan State Police."

Dispatch replied, "This is MSP, go ahead Iron River Command."

The chief replied, "Have the ambulances still come in, but stage them at the Iron River Police Headquarters. We found both officers. Both officers are down. Killed in action."

There was a brief pause from dispatch for a few moments. Then dispatch said, "Message received, Command. We are sorry. All responsible parties will be notified. MSP troopers are en route. ETA ten minutes. Crystal Falls PD is sending some help as well. Their ETA including the ambulances is seven minutes."

The chief stood up and replied, said, "Message received. Have all responding units meet my officers at Iron River Police Headquarters."

"What are we going to do, Chief? We can't just leave our own out here!" Bobby said, trying to collect his composure.

In a trembling voice, the chief replied, "At least we know where the remains are located. The beast won't be back. He likes bodies when they are still warm. Believe me, I know. Let's walk together back to the street. You take your squad car over to the church and talk to your dad. Also, get a hold of those kids' parents. Tell them that you'll drop them off at their homes. I'll be on the phone with all of our off-duty officers. They will be emergency recalled."

Bobby looked at the chief puzzled, and said, "What are you going to do, Chief?"

The chief answered, "I'll wait next to the squad cars on the street and keep watch over the town."

As they walked back to the squad cars, the chief kept watch as Bobby drove off toward the church.

CHAPTER 27

....

THE HISTORY EXPLAINED

The group were all frightened beyond the point of understanding what was happening. The beast followed them for miles! The illusion of safety that they all felt throughout most of their lives was now unraveled. Rita was crying and shaking. Ryan was catching his breath as he fell to the floor. Robert was in disbelief. He couldn't believe that the legend of werewolves was true. Mike who previously seemed tough and calm was now trembling. Mr. Rosalie was with the group. Liam felt at least somewhat safe with Mr. Rosalie. He definitely came off as a protective guardian figure. Mr. Rosalie walked down the church aisle toward everyone and said, "It's okay, kids. It's okay. Like Angela said, you'll be safe here."

Ryan turned to Mr. Rosalie and said, "Who the hell is Angela? The old lady who opened the door?"

"That's right, dear," Angela said. "I'm sorry, where are my manners? My name is Angela Miller. And yes you'll be safe here. The beast will not enter this place. We have protection here."

Mike looked up at Angela and said, "What are you saying? That thing is afraid of religious things like holy water and crosses?"

Robert chimed up and said, "No, you idiot. That's vampires. Werewolves don't like silver."

Mike replied, "Hey, you little jerk. The old lady just said that—"

Nick interjected, "Just like Angela said, you'll be safe here. But the young man here is right. The fact that we are in a church makes no difference. It's the layers of protection that are built around the church that's important."

Angela nodded. "The large cross outside the church here is made completely of silver. All the crosses around this church are silver, and the church grounds are surrounded by wolf's-bane. The silver for the crosses came from the workers in the mines. My family worked in the mines for years. That's where I got this." Angela held up the silver cross that she wore around her neck. "This cross is also made of silver from the same mines. It's been passed down in my family for generations."

Mike looked baffled at the revelation of this information, turned to Mr. Rosalie and Mrs. Miller and said, "You mean to tell me you have a history with that thing? How long have you known about its existence?"

Mr. Rosalie and Mrs. Miller looked at each other. Mrs. Miller walked toward us. Mr. Rosalie said, "It's been a long time...but maybe we should—"

Angela interjected, "The cat is out of the bag, dear. No need trying to cover up anymore."

With a brief pause and a sigh, Angela continued, "The story of the beast goes back to long before my family first settled in the area. And granted, my family was one of the first families to settle and help establish the town. At one time, this area was Native American Territory. The local tribes, Menominee and Ojibwe, have lived in this area for hundreds of years. They stayed in this area for generations because of its excellent hunting and fishing grounds. As the town was established and the legal battle over the ownership of the land continued, the tribes made a legal agreement to settle in their main hunting grounds along the wilderness area where your grandfather disappeared. There were tales about people going missing and being found half eaten throughout the history in this area. Mind you this was long before science and technology were so advanced. One summer in particular was quite gruesome.

"At the time, I was a young nurse working at the local hospital in the emergency room. One early morning, a hunting party of five men came into the ER. They were all World War II veterans. Most of them were bloody and injured, but they had enough energy to carry a fallen hunter whose throat was fatally cut by several large claw marks. That hunter was pronounced dead on arrival. We did our duty tending to the injured hunters when the police arrived.

At the time, our current chief of police was a young rookie beat cop. He was taking statements from one of the hunters while I was tending to his wounds. I remember the hunter saying, 'We were hunting just outside the wilderness when we were attacked by a hairy monster. We were sleeping in our camp, and we were suddenly attacked during the early morning hours. We tried to use our military training to survive. Ambush tactic. But it was no use. Our weapons were useless!'"

There was a brief pause while Angela collected her thoughts. Mike looked up to Angela and questioned, "So what happened next?"

Angela continued, "After statements were taken, the police followed up with their investigation. They were assuming that the hunters were disorientated and confused, given the conditions, and they were attacked by a large black bear. Our local police and the state police decided to conduct an investigation into the wilderness and talk to the local tribe chiefs. The local chiefs wanted to help with the investigation and also kill the beast once and for all. The police were baffled by the tribe telling their legendary tales of the werewolf. Although they didn't believe most of the local legend, they still decided to hunt for the beast regardless of tales, believing they were hunting a man-eating bear. The police called upon local help from hunters and the Native American tribes. Nick was a part of that hunting party. So was Mr. Schubert and his brother. They waited until the next full moon to hunt the beast under the direction of the local tribes. The tribes advised the hunting party to use silver bullets, but that was immediately dismissed. Some say they found the beast, but most of us know that the beast found the hunting party. The werewolf attacked and took the party completely by surprise. It killed tribal hunters who were armed with silver-tipped spears and arrows, none of whom were able to make a fatal hit with their weapons. The police and our local hunters used their firearms, but they didn't work. During the attack, Mr. Schubert's brother was killed along with a young state trooper. Mr. Schubert dropped his rifle and grabbed a silver-tipped spear off of the ground. He moved quickly toward the beast from a blindside and made a fatal piercing hit with the spear right into its chest. Before the beast collapsed, it reached down and bit Mr. Schubert in the shoulder. The beast was killed. We didn't know it at the time, but the curse of the werewolf was transferred to him."

Nick chimed in saying, "Wait! What? You mean to tell me that old man Schubert is the…?"

Angela replied, "Yes, dear. You figured that maybe the beast never died, and we never finished the job. The beast died, but the curse lived on. We took Mr. Schubert back to the hospital where he was treated for his wounds. In total, four men were killed during the hunt. Two tribal hunters, a state trooper, and Mr. Schubert's brother. After he healed we, Chief Patterson and I, brought him to the tribal chiefs in the wilderness. They warned us that the curse of the werewolf was now transferred to Mr. Schubert. The only suggestions they gave to end the curse was either murder or suicide. This was far out of the question. Chief Patterson, Mr. Schubert, and I came up with a plan. Mr. Schubert was very familiar with the old mines since his family owned most of them. There was an old abandoned building on the outskirts of the Ottawa National Forest near one of the old mines. It was a meeting and collection area for mining materials in the area. During the monthly periods of full and new moons, Mr. Schubert would drive himself out to that old building and barricade himself inside of it, far from anyone, and stay there until the following morning."

The group couldn't believe what they were hearing. The story and the pieces of the puzzle were finally coming together. Liam looked at Mrs. Miller and asked, "So, he's been doing this since that time? What has changed between now and then?"

Angela collected her thoughts and said, "Yes. He's lived with this curse for a long time. Every full moon and new moon, he drives out to that abandoned building, chains himself up, and waits for the full transformation from man into beast. In exchange for keeping this dark secret, Mr. Schubert annually donates large sums of money to the town and the surrounding community in order to help the area flourish. The money was also used to make certain safeguards like the silver cross outside and the wolf's-bane surrounding certain areas of the town and communities. I believe as Mr. Schubert has grown old he has lost his control over the beast. When he was younger his full transformation would only happen during the full and new moon cycles. According to the sequence of events, we now believe that he transforms more often, and it's now less predictable. This month in particular is the time when the beast grows stronger. This is after the harvest moon. This is considered the Halloween moon."

Mike asked Mrs. Miller, "So, during the October moons the beast is at its strongest? Great! What do we do now?"

Angela and Nick stood silent as a police squad car pulled up to the front of the building. They heard a car door slam shut and someone running up the church stairs. It was Bobby. He banged on the door yelling at the group to open it. They all ran toward the door as Mr. Rosalie pulled the group back and said, "Please, kids, let me do it!"

Nick opened the door as his son ran inside. Bobby looked at his father and exclaimed, "Dad! What the hell is going on? We have officers down! That thing killed them! The chief is out there on the street guarding the town. He said to come here and help you and these kids!"

Angela nodded, looked at Bobby's long rifle, and said, "Okay, young man. Did the chief tell you what kind of bullets are in those long rifles?"

Bobby answered, "He said silver bullets! He said we're dealing with….with….with—"

Nick interjected, "Yes, Son. It's a werewolf. I know."

Bobby, shocked by his father's answer, replied, "Then you know? How? What? What are we going to do?"

CHAPTER 28

....

DO YOU HAVE ANY IDEA
WHAT TIME IT IS?

As the group stood in the church lobby, Liam's phone was lighting up. He looked down at his phone and said, "Oh crap. It's my mom. She's probably really mad. We haven't checked in for a while."

Mr. Rosalie looked at Liam and asked, "Your parents are calling, sonny?"

Liam looked up at Nick and nodded yes.

Nick replied, "Answer the phone and talk to her for a minute, and then let me talk to her."

Liam agreed and answered. "Hi, Mom. What's up?"

Annie exclaimed, "What's up! What's up! I'll tell you what's up! You've been gone all day with those friends of yours. You haven't checked in for a long time. We were starting to worry about you. While we were watching TV an emergency broadcast came over the TV and on our phones saying that an emergency shelter-in-place order is now in effect for the town of Iron River by the order of the chief of police. Your father is on the internet trying to figure out what's going on! Some people posted videos of police pointing their guns at something while people were running all around Main Street!"

Mr. Rosalie could hear Liam's mother yelling through the phone loud and clear. He signaled to Liam as he handed over the phone. Liam figured Mr. Rosalie could help explain the situation.

Nick grabbed the phone and said, "Hello? Hello? Ma'am? Is this Annie?"

Annie answered, "Yes this is Annie. Who the hell is this?"

Nick answered, "Ma'am, this is Nick Rosalie. The owner of the antique shop. You know, Bobby's father. Your son and his friends are safe and sound. Bobby is here with me at the church."

Annie replied, "The church? What the hell is he doing at a church at this time of night? You better explain to me what the hell is going on!"

Mr. Rosalie turned to Liam and said, "Is she usually like this?"

Liam answered, "Only when she's mad at me or Boo or when my dad buys a lot of stuff on the internet."

Nick continued, "Ma'am, Bobby and I are going to escort the kids home immediately. We will explain when we arrive, okay?"

Annie replied, "Okay. This better be good, Mr. Rosalie, or that young man and his friends will never be allowed to hang out up here anymore!"

Annie ended the call, and Liam asked, "Okay. Are we seriously leaving now? How are we going to do this?"

Nick looked at everyone and Bobby and said, "Bobby, you stay here with the kids. I'll go get this young man's jeep. When I get back I'll ride with you, Son, and we will escort these kids back home and talk to their parents. Do you have the keys, sonny?"

Mike reached into his pocket and handed the keys over to Nick and said, "Please be careful with it."

Nick replied, "Will do. I'll be back in a minute."

Bobby grabbed his dad's arm and said, "Dad! You're not going to just walk all the way down Main Street by yourself. Let me go."

Nick pulled away from his son and said, "It's okay, Son. You stay here. I'll be fine. I have to talk to the chief."

Nick walked down the now quiet and deserted Main Street. He looked around and up toward the full moon high above the night's sky. The moon had a slight orange glow to it. Nick only saw movement near the police squad cars' barricade. Chief Patterson was on the phone while he kept watch over the town. As Nick walked closer to the chief, he overheard the chief saying, "Yes, that's correct. We will need the state police here while my officers and some officers from Crystal Falls PD go out and hunt this thing. ETA is two minutes? Okay. Message received. Thank you."

As the chief ended his call, he saw Nick. "Hey, Nick! Bobby with those kids at the church?"

Nick answered, "That's right, Chief."

Chief Patterson nodded. He reached down into his trunk and pulled out another long rifle. The chief handed the rifle over to Nick and said, "You might need one of these."

Nick took the rifle and said, "Thanks, Chief. I'll take the young man's jeep back over to the church. Bobby and I will escort the kids home. Afterward, we figure we can come back and help you. Have you seen anything?"

The chief replied, "Nothing. Been looking all over the place, but I can't find it. Looks like it vanished into the darkness. Figure its making its way back to the wilderness. ETA for state police and Crystal Falls PD is a couple of minutes. We have to finish this thing, Nick."

Nick said, "It? You mean old man Schubert, don't you Chief?"

Chief Patterson replied, "Angela told you."

Nick answered, "Yes she did. All of this time, Chief. I've known you my whole life and you couldn't tell me."

Chief Patterson answered, "Nick, I'm sorry. Angela and I both agreed that the fewer people who know the better."

Nick replied, "Damn it, Rich. We could have taken care of this problem years ago."

Chief Patterson exclaimed, "Schubert has helped the local community thrive over the decades! If it weren't for him, I don't know if this town would have survived."

Nick exclaimed, "How's that survival looking now, Rich? We have a town of good people running into their homes and locking it down. This is a town where most people don't even lock their doors."

Chief Patterson shook his head and continued, "Nick, we did what we had to do in order to protect our little world in this small corner of Michigan. What's done is done. But I guarantee you that we will finish this now!"

Both men agreed, and a short discussion continued as a wave of police squad cars with lights and sirens made their way down the hills of Route 2 from the east toward Iron River. Nick looked at the chief as he started up the jeep and said, "You do what you have to do. I'll meet up with you as soon as I can. He's lost control, Rich. We have to finish it now!"

Nick drove off toward the church as the wave of squad cars were now entering Main Street. Nick pulled up to the church as the group waited by the front door. They filed outside and ran toward the jeep. Bobby walked alongside them with his rifle pointed and scanning the area. Angela stood at the threshold of the church entrance. Liam looked back at Mrs. Miller and said, "Are coming with us, Mrs. Miller?"

Angela looked down at Liam with her silver cross in her hand and said, "No, dear. I'll be safe here until morning." She looked down at her silver cross. "My husband and I were not blessed with children. I'm the last one, and I lived my life. Take this, dear. It will protect you as it protected my family." She handed him the silver cross.

Liam said, "Thank you, Mrs. Miller. I promise to take care of it."

She replied, "As long as you take care of it, it will take care of you. Now, go home to your family. Tell your grandparents I wish them well."

They loaded into the jeep as Nick walked over to Bobby's squad car. Nick turned back to the group and said, "You kids start driving; we will be right behind you the whole way."

Mike did exactly what Nick instructed him to do. By now the wave of police cars drove past the church and were now parked near the chief. Mike turned onto Route 2 as Bobby and Nick rode behind. They were all so incredibly nervous. The nights here were not so illuminated as they were back home. They traveled down Route 2 and turned down Sunset Valley Lake Road. They were surrounded by darkness while they drove down the winding two-lane road. The group all kept close watch on their surroundings. They could never tell if or when the beast would return from beyond the darkness. The one reassurance Liam had was hearing the sounds of nature continue throughout the night. Liam remembered his first encounter with the beast. It struck him how the nightly creatures either ran away or fell deeply silent when the beast approached.

Within a few minutes, they pulled up to their driveway where their family was waiting outside. Even in the darkness Liam could see how angry both his parents were at the time. They were waiting there with Mike and Rita's mother and grandmother. Daniel and Tina stayed inside the house, keeping watch over Boo, as she already was fast asleep. They all exited the jeep, and surprisingly, Liam's parents gave him hugs. Mike and Rita were also greeted by their mom and grandmother with a warm embrace. Rita didn't let go of her mom, and she started to cry in her arms. Annie said, "Thank God you're home safe. I'm mad but it's because I was so worried about you. We were all worried. Now, is someone going to explain just what exactly happened tonight?"

Just then, Nick and Bobby exited the squad car with their rifles slung over their shoulders. Will exclaimed, "Bobby and Mr. Rosalie! What the hell are those things for?"

Nick and Bobby both looked at each other as Nick answered, "Protection! It's best to explain all of this inside the house. Come on everyone, inside right now!"

Will was baffled by their serious tone. "Bobby, what the hell is going on?"

Bobby replied, "You all heard him. From what I've seen tonight, I don't know if these rifles will be enough. But let's get inside. Dad will explain everything."

Everyone filed into the house and quickly locked the door.

CHAPTER 29

....

THE CAVALRY HAS ARRIVED

The parade of police squad cars entered Main Street in Iron River. It was a mixture of police ranging from county sheriffs, state police, and the neighboring city of Crystal Falls. The sound of the sirens was deafening, and the sight of all of the lights from their cruisers helped illuminate the surrounding side streets just off of the main road. Chief Patterson stood by his vehicle and gestured with a hand signal to have all of the police officers silence their sirens. The front car in this parade was a longtime friend and colleague, the Crystal Falls Police Department Chief of Police Mr. Steven Wellington. He was the first to exit his squad car and approach Chief Patterson. Chief Wellington was an older gentleman just like Chief Patterson. He was a seasoned veteran who grew up in Crystal Falls and started his career shortly after Chief Patterson started his career in Iron River. He was a short, kind, soft-spoken man with silver hair parted on his right side and heavy large glasses resting on his nose.

As Chief Wellington approached Chief Patterson to shake his hand, he said, "Howdy, Rich! Seems like you guys have had one hell of a night around here. Is it what I think it is?"

Chief Patterson extended his hand warmly toward Chief Wellington while still holding his long rifle in his other hand. "Unfortunately yes! Let me talk to the rest of the cavalry and then I'll talk to you privately. Old man Schubert has lost control, Steven. Killed two officers already tonight!"

Chief Wellington was shocked and sympathetic when hearing the news. He replied, "You do what you got to do, Chief. I'll be here waiting for you."

As all the officers exited their cars, they approached Chief Patterson and formed a semicircle similar to their roll calls. One of the officers approached the chief. He was a captain with the Michigan State Police. His name was Scottie Weber. Scottie shook Chief Patterson's hand. "Chief! Nice to meet you, sir. Without skipping too much of the pleasantries, it's my understanding that one of my officers is down, is that correct?"

Chief Patterson looked down at his feet and said, "It's my unfortunate duty to inform you that's correct, Captain. One of my officers and I checked him for signs of life after the attack. He lost too much blood and was beyond the point of possibly being viable. I am sorry. I have the ambulances staging until we secured the scene. Your trooper's body, along with one of my sergeants, is two blocks west of here just outside of town along the woods. I made sure to mark the crime scene before coming back up here."

Captain Weber was saddened by the news. He replied, "He was a good young trooper. Strong, brave, honest, and a family man with just a couple of years on the job. I never had to make a death notification before. I hoped and prayed I would never have to." Captain Weber paused for a moment as he started to get choked up and upset. He gathered his composure and asked Chief Patterson, "What the hell happened?"

Chief Patterson looked over to Chief Wellington. Neither of them said a word. Chief Patterson knew what he had to do.

Chief Patterson grabbed his bull horn out of his squad car and climbed on top of the hood of his car. He now had his long rifle swung over his shoulder, the bull horn in one hand, and the mic in the other. He said, "Evening, Officers. Thank you for coming as quickly as you could. Here's the situation. A state trooper and one of my officers were involved in a high-speed pursuit and a roadblock with a young group of kids driving quickly along Route 2. When they pulled over the kids they were both attacked by a giant black bear!"

Chief Patterson paused and looked over to Chief Wellington. Chief Wellington was nodding his head in approval as Chief Patterson continued, "Both were killed and dragged just outside of town. We need your help securing the town and performing a search up and down our neighborhood streets. I want our families to feel as safe as they can. By first light, some of my Iron River officers along with some help from Crystal Falls PD will accompany me and assist with searching for this creature. We are very familiar with this surrounding area. State police, I will need your help with evidence collection from the crime scene. County sheriffs, we will need you to stay at our police station until we come back from our mission. Some of my officers are being recalled as we speak. They will help patrol the area. I'll answer questions as they come, but please direct your questions to your chain of command."

Captain Weber grabbed a few of his troopers and directed them over to the gory scene of the fallen officers. County sheriffs moved their units to the police station. Some Crystal Falls officers entered their cars and began their patrol of the town. A few Crystal Falls officers stayed near Chief Wellington as he directed them to perform various duties and off they went. Chief Patterson was now alone with Chief Wellington. Chief Wellington turned to Chief Patterson and said, "A black bear. That sounds a little too far-fetched, but I think it will work. For now at least. So, Chief, what is our first move?"

Chief Patterson replied, "I have a pretty good idea where that bastard went. Only God knows if he has any control over the beast when he transforms. If he has some control, he might go back to his home or back to that abandoned building deep in the wilderness. It will be dawn in a few hours. I say you and me head over to his place. Do a search there first."

Chief Wellington approved of this plan and asked, "So if we find him, we are finally ending this, yes?"

Chief Patterson answered, "We have no choice. What will be next? We have a small town and a lot of young families here."

Chief Wellington went to his trunk and pulled out his long rifle. He pulled a flap down and out came a box full of silver bullets. Chief Patterson walked over to Chief Wellington's trunk and asked, "Are you ready for this, Steven?"

Chief Wellington looked at Chief Patterson with a serious look and said, "I've worried about this secret for years. We covered up a lot of stuff over the years, Rich. The natives call it a curse, and it is…truly. Let's finish it. After tonight, no more!"

They both entered their squad cars. Chief Wellington pulled up to Chief Patterson and asked, "So first stop, the old Schubert mansion?"

Chief Patterson replied, "Yup. That's the first stop. It's the closest safe haven for that bastard. Let's roll!"

CHAPTER 30

....

HOW LONG HAS HE BEEN LIVING LIKE THIS?

Two police squad cars raced east along Route 2. They made a sharp left turn onto Sunset Valley Lake Road. The dark and winding road illuminated as the squad cars sped toward the Schubert family mansion. It had been a long night already. So long in fact it was the early morning hours now. Fog started to lift off the lake and flood the road. Chief Patterson sipped on his coffee and listened to his scanner as he navigated his vehicle to his destination. They both pulled into the long half-circle driveway of the Schubert estate. The sight was spooky to say the least. The estate was dark without any sign of anyone being home. The cool October night was lit up by the moon tracking along the night sky. By now, the area was anxiously quiet. The only noise was the sounds of frogs echoing throughout the bushes and high grass, and the fish eating along the surface of the water.

Chief Patterson and Chief Wellington both exited their vehicles, each grabbing their long rifles and flashlights. Chief Patterson knocked at the front door and rang the doorbell several times. No answer. Chief Patterson exclaimed, "Mr. Schubert. This is Chief Patterson. We need to speak to you immediately!" The first course of action was left with no answer or reply.

Chief Wellington said, "Any thoughts on how we want to do this, Rich?"

Chief Patterson replied, "Well, I figure the moon will be gone soon. But the setting moon might also mean that he is losing his power. Basically, I figure we just do it live and see what happens, Steven."

Chief Wellington smiled and said, "Keeping it old school and simple. Just balls, rifles, and common sense. Like that plan. I don't know about you, but my door-kicking days are long over. Figure maybe we search the exterior first. See if we can see anyone and look for an easy way inside. Most of these lake house deals have glass doors on the back portion of the house."

Chief Patterson replied, "Sounds like a plan to me. Let's stay together. Clockwise search around the house."

Chief Wellington cocked back his rifle and said, "Let's go hunting, Rich!"

They each started to do their 360-degree search of the estate. With their long rifles at their sides, they used their flashlights to search up and down and back and forth toward the house and its surrounding grounds. They both made their way to the back section of the house that overlooked the lake. Chief Patterson shined his flashlight at the ground, and he stumbled across the large firepit area near the corner of the property. As Chief Patterson shined his light at the pit, he said, "Steven, take a look at this. Shine your light on the pit!"

Chief Wellington asked, "Why? What's up, Rich?"

Chief Patterson replied, "Just look, Steven. Looks like old man Schubert wasn't just burning old timber, twigs, and leaves. It looks like a pair of glasses and some particles of old clothes!"

Chief Wellington exclaimed, "Good lord. Probably burning evidence." Chief Wellington pointed his rifle and flashlight toward the estate's back entrance and continued, "The glass sliding door should be our easiest way into the house. I'll just have to break one side and lift the locking mechanism. Looks like there's a security system attached to it. You want me to call it in?"

Chief Patterson answered, "I'll take care of it. Let's plan on that."

Chief Patterson and Chief Wellington moved up to the sliding door as Chief Patterson began to talk into his radio saying, "Iron River Command to County Sheriff at Police HQ?"

A voice replied and said, "Yeah, Chief. This is County Sheriff at your HQ. Go ahead with your message."

Chief Patterson answered, "Yeah County, we are going to force entry into the Schubert estate out at Sunset Valley Lake. When the security company calls into HQ tell them to disregard the alarm. This is a police matter."

The voice replied from the radio, "Message received, Chief."

Within a minute, the glass door was busted and both Chief Patterson and Chief Wellington made their way into the structure. They entered the kitchen area after crossing the threshold of the sliding door. The alarm was immediately activated. They pointed their weapons and flashlights further into the house. No movement. Chief Patterson began to talk loudly into his radio as Chief Wellington kept his rifle pointed down into the long hallways of the estate. Chief Patterson exclaimed, "Iron River Command to HQ. Have the alarm company deactivate the alarm!"

Dispatch replied, "Message received, Chief! We are talking to the alarm company now. They will silence the alarm remotely."

Within a few seconds the loud security alarm silenced. Chief Patterson said, "Well, that's better. I got that ringing in my ears."

Chief Wellington replied, "I almost had to turn down my hearing aid. Like I said, I ain't the young beat cop who still kicks in doors."

Chief Patterson answered, "You and me both, Steven. What is that horrible smell? Smells like wild animals live in here!"

"You're telling me. Been in a lot of messed up places in my day. This is one horrific smell. Also smells like death in here!"

They continued their search inside the structure. There was no movement and no sound. The large hallways and rooms that emptied into them were filled with old furniture, which was now shrouded by old sheets and moth balls. As they made their sweeps in and out of rooms, Chief Wellington questioned, "Are you sure old man Schubert still lives in this house? Seems like no one has lived here in years."

Chief Patterson answered, "I'm sure. Angela Miller still keeps tabs on him. She checks in with me from time to time."

"Floor is clear. There are stairs that lead either down to the lower level or up toward the bedrooms. What do you want to search first?"

Chief Patterson answered, "I have a feeling. A bad feeling about the lower level. Let's check that out next."

They both made their way down the stairs. Chief Patterson was in front with his rifle and flashlight facing in front of him. Chief Wellington was behind him sweeping his rifle and flashlight back and forth along the rear. As they reached the bottom step, the smell of wild animals and death only got heavier. Enough so that both chiefs started to cough and gag. It was pitch black in the basement. No light whatsoever. Chief Patterson turned his light toward a small basement window that had been concealed with old newspapers. He found a light switch and turned on the lights overlooking the hallway. The lights illuminated the gruesome display in front of them. The lights showed a large room and a long corridor. Large claw and bite marks littered the walls and ceiling. Trails of blood made the floor slippery and sticky. Chief Patterson exclaimed, "Sweet Jesus. Holy Mary Mother of God!"

Chief Wellington replied as he coughed and gaged, "Agreed, Rich. Well that explains the smell."

"Yes indeed, Steven. How long has he been living like this? Only God knows. I hate to do it, but we have to check those rooms along the hallway."

They each made their way carefully down the hallway. Both didn't want to slip and fall into the carnage just below their boots. They both pointed their weapons toward the end of the hallway. Chief Wellington occasionally shined his light behind him to check their rear. At the end of the hallway, there were two doors, one of the left side and the other on the right. Chief Patterson reached the back doors and said, "Okay, Steven. Which one to we check first?"

Chief Wellington said, "I fear we won't like what lurks behind both of these doors so just pick one. I'll watch the rear."

Chief Patterson replied, "Left door first it is!"

The door wasn't locked. He opened the door and discovered what was stored on the other side of it. Chief Patterson flipped on a light switch, which startled some movement. Chief Patterson yelled, "What the hell?"

Chief Wellington exclaimed, "What the hell now?"

"Look, Steven."

The large room was divided into a corridor in the middle and shelves and cages along each side. On the right side were shelves of cold storage canned goods. One shelf was filled with blood-stained hunting rifles and other small arms weapons and hunting knives. On the left side were several large dog cages, and each was filled with wild living animals! They walked down the corridor. A couple of cages had some young deer. Others had several rabbits. One had a family of loons. "What do make of this, Rich?" Chief Wellington questioned as he looked in amazement.

Chief Patterson answered, "Maybe he would feed on these animals during his transformation! Something to satisfy the beast within!"

Chief Wellington replied, "Good God! Now the real question, what's behind door number 2?"

Chief Patterson answered, "Only one way to find out."

They exited the room and made their way to the other door across the hallway. Both their breathing and heartrates were racing. The door seemed to be made of metal frame and body. "What do you make of this, Steven?" Chief Patterson questioned.

"Seen all types of doors. This one is heavily reinforced. If it's locked we will need the fire department out here to help force entry. It's an inward-swinging door with automatic locking mechanisms on the outward hallway side. It's certainly meant to keep something inside of it."

Chief Patterson tried the handle. It was unlocked! Before he opened, he signaled to Chief Wellington to have his weapon at the ready. Chief Patterson open the door and they both quickly entered with their rifles pointed at the ready. The room was a gruesome scene. In the large room were the remains of several small animals. Mainly deer, rabbits, and coyotes. All of which had been half eaten and left to rot on the floor. There were no windows. All of the walls were made of reinforced metal. In the center of the room was a metal chair. The chair was in horrific condition with old blood stains and several claw marks and bites. From an anchored position in the base of the outer facing wall, there were several long steel chains with locking mechanisms meant to secure extremities!

Chief Patterson and Chief Wellington looked in amazement at the carnage of this hellish environment. After a few moments of stunned uncomfortable silence, Chief Patterson said, "Time to get out of here, Steven! He's not here. We will need help from a forensic team to examine the firepit outside. I have a bad feeling that those items belonged to that retired state trooper who went hunting in the wilderness. I'll make the call to have them come out here by first light."

Chief Wellington replied, "You know that the forensic team will want to investigate the inside of the house too. How do we explain this?"

Chief Patterson answered, "We are way beyond trying to cover up this story anymore, Steven. It will be up to old man Schubert to explain himself if he comes in alive."

CHAPTER 31

....

POSSIBLE DEATH NOTIFICATION SENT OUT

It was now dawn as the sun rose over Iron River. It was a cool October morning. The early morning dew was frosty as the overnight temperatures dropped just below freezing. On a typical holiday weekend, Iron River would be a busy beehive of activity. Fisherman would be on the move and making their way to the boat launches. Families with their campers would be packing up and making their way to and from various camps in the area. On this particular morning, the only movement in and around town were vehicles with lights and sirens attached to them. Normal citizens took the warnings seriously and stayed in their homes. Several state police squad cars were making their way from the overnight crime scene. They were now making their way east on Route 2 and turning onto Sunset Valley Lake Road.

This was the forensic team that Chief Patterson requested just a couple of hours prior to their arrival. Chief Patterson and Chief Wellington were waiting outside the Schubert family mansion in order to secure the scene and await their arrival. As the squad cars pulled up, Chief Patterson approached the team while Chief Wellington waited near the firepit. As they exited their vehicles, the team gathered their necessary tools and equipment and were greeted by Chief Patterson. He addressed them saying, "Good morning to all of you, and thank you for coming. I know you've already had a horrific night, but we need your help with this one. Chief Wellington is along the side of the property waiting for you next to a firepit. I called the local judge in the area early this morning. He gave us a warrant to search the entire property inside and out. First to the outside."

The forensic team walked with Chief Patterson toward the firepit as he continued saying, "We have remains of personal items in this firepit. I don't know for sure, but I believe they belong to a hunter who was a retired state trooper that went missing recently. Looks like the homeowner tried to burn some evidence but didn't finish the job. After we secure the evidence, I would like for you to transfer custody of the glasses over to me so I can bring them to his wife. Maybe she will be able to tell me for sure."

The forensic team went to work. Marking and securing evidence as they found it on the property. After they properly secured the glasses, they brought them over to Chief Patterson and transferred custody to him. Chief Patterson and Chief Wellington were both walking with each other around the property to see if they could find any other evidence during the daytime. Both chiefs walked back over to the forensic team as they were finishing their work along the firepit.

Chief Wellington said, "Chief Patterson and I walked the rest of the property. Couldn't find anything else out of sorts. The inside, however, is definitely something completely out of sorts. I recommend working in shifts. The smell is God-awful, and the scene is quite gruesome, especially on the lower level. We will request animal control out here to help secure the live wild animals inside the property."

The forensic team looked baffled by his comments on wild animals as the chief continued saying, "Don't worry. It will make more sense once you go in. Chief Patterson and I forced entry into the structure through that sliding glass door on the back side of the estate. From there we made our search. If you have any questions, you now have our phone numbers. We won't be far. Just the other side of the lake to talk to Larry's wife, Gabby. The missing person in question. Thank you."

Chief Patterson and Chief Wellington walked back to their squad cars together. Chief Patterson look at Chief Wellington and said, "I feel bad for the forensic team. They have their work cut out for them."

Chief Wellington replied, "They'll be fine. Most of the kids look young. Forget about them, and let's go to talk to that wife. I bet you she probably feels worse."

Chief Patterson replied, "You may be right, Steven. Let's get there."

They both got inside their cars and drove off with lights and sirens to the opposite end of the lake.

Will was up all night with Bobby. As dawn approached, they watched the activity at the Schubert family estate from the family's pier. Will and Bobby were both drinking their coffee and sitting on the bench at the end of the pier. Will turned to Bobby and said, "Jesus, Bobby. You've heard me say it a few times but I'll say it again. Thank you for making sure my boy and his friends got home safe."

Bobby replied, "No worries, brother. Just doing my job, and I know you would have done the same for my family heaven forbid."

Will nodded in approval. "I'm just happy the boys and rest of the family were able to get some sleep after last night. I don't know if I could. I had everyone stay inside the house. No one stayed in the camper last night. So you're for real. A real-life werewolf! The silver bullets, full moons, teeth, hair, and claws. The whole thing right out of a movie!"

Bobby nodded sadly and said, "I'm afraid so, Will. I'm afraid so. Seems like Chief Patterson knew about this for quite some time and kept it under wraps."

Bobby and Will watched the squad cars speed off toward them from the other side of the lake. Bobby and Will both stood up as Bobby reached for his radio. Before he could speak into it he heard Chief Patterson calling for him saying, "Iron River Command to Squad 3. Bobby, are you still at the house across the lake?"

Bobby answered, "Squad 3 to Iron River Command, yes that's correct, Chief."

Chief Patterson replied, "Okay good. Wait for me to arrive. I'm on my way to you with Chief Wellington from Crystal Falls. Looks like we have to talk to Larry's wife."

Bobby answered, "Message received, Chief."

Will looked at Bobby as he overheard the radio messages saying, "What do you think happened, Bobby?"

Bobby replied, "I hate to say it but I think that forensic team found something of Larry's in and around the property. This may lead to a possible death notification."

Will replied, "Oh no! That poor woman and her family have been through so much already. What can I do to help?"

Bobby answered, "You've been around a lot of sad scenes with your job, Will. More so than mine. Just be there to support the family. I think they will need it."

Chief Patterson and Chief Wellington both pulled into the driveway. As they exited their cars, Chief Patterson held a clear bag with official marking outside of it. Inside were the pair of glasses. Both of the chiefs approached Bobby and Will. Chief Patterson began saying, "Morning, Bobby. Good work last night, son. I'm glad you got those kids home safe."

Bobby replied, "Yes, sir. My father and I stayed with the family for a little while explaining the situation. After some time, my dad and I rode around the area looking for it. Couldn't find anything. I dropped my dad off at his house and then came back here this morning."

Chief Patterson replied, "Seems like everyone has had a long night."

The chiefs looked at Will. They were both unfamiliar with the man. Bobby looked at his friend and back at the chiefs saying, "Chief Patterson and Chief Wellington, this is Will. His family has a vacation home here next door to Larry and Gabby. He's a buddy of mine you may remember I mentioned to you, Chief. He's a firefighter from Chicago."

Chief Patterson and Chief Wellington both extended their hands and greeted Will. Chief Patterson said, "Chicago! Far from home aren't you? Bobby says this is your family's place?"

Will answered, "Yes, sir. My wife's side. We try to come up here when we can. We figure getting out to the country and finding some peace and quiet will be good for the family. Little did we know…"

Chief Patterson replied, "Indeed. Yes Indeed. Steven and Bobby with me please. Let's get this over with."

Bobby, Chief Patterson, and Chief Wellington all started walking toward Gabby's house. By now the commotion in the driveway led to movement in the household. Gabby was the first to exit the house. Both Mike and Mike's mother walked with Gabby to greet the officer. Gabby began speaking saying, "You know something don't you? Is it Larry? Is he dead? Please just tell me!"

Chief Patterson looked at the other officers and began saying in a comforting voice, "Ma'am, first we don't know for certain if Larry is alive or dead. But…but it's my unfortunate duty to inform you that we have a high index of suspicion that Larry is dead."

Gabby gasped as she held on to her family saying, "Oh God! I knew it! What did you find?"

Chief Patterson held up the clear sealed bag from his hand and said, "Gabby, we found these glasses. Do you think they are Larry's?"

Gabby grabbed the bag and looked at its contents. As she examined them she began to cry. She said, "Those are my Larry's glasses for sure. I would clean them almost every night. He hasn't changed his frame in years." She dropped the bag onto the ground and began to cry more as she immediately wrapped herself around her family for comfort. Her family helped bring her back into the house. As the officers were walking back toward their squad cars, Mike ran out to them saying, "So what's the next move? What do we do next?"

Chief Patterson answered, "The next move is to try to find Mr. Schubert and bring him in for questioning."

Mike exclaimed, "Questioning! How can you question or reason with a rampaging beast! We have to hunt this bastard down and shoot him on sight!"

Chief replied in a serious tone saying, "Son, listen. There is no *we* in this scenario. *We* implies that you're going to help us in our matters. And there is something called proper police procedure. We have this situation under control. Your place is here with your family."

Mike replied angrily, "That's a complete load of crap! You don't have anything handled. If you did that bastard would be dead at the morgue just like those officers from last night!"

Will walked over and interjected, "Mike! Young man, please let these officers do their job!"

Mike replied, "Yeah whatever man. It's not your family! Your family is all safe! My family will never be whole again because of that monster!" Mike ran back into his house and slammed the door shut.

CHAPTER 32

....

WE HAVE TO TALK
TO THE NATIVES

Chief Patterson picked up the clear sealed evidence bag off of the ground and began to walk back to his squad car. The other men followed after him. As he reached the car, he said, "Well, this is the part of the job I always hated. Still do. If you ever get used to it, then it's time to retire."

Bobby shook his head in approval and asked Chief Patterson, "What's next, Chief?"

Chief Patterson answered, "For now, Bobby, why don't you go home and get some rest. I have to go back to the station with Chief Wellington."

Will looked at the officer and asked, "Anything I can do to help, gentlemen?"

Chief Patterson looked at Will and said, "I appreciate that, Will. And honestly if we can use the help I'll have Bobby contact you. For now, just make sure you stay with your family. When are you planning to leave for Chicago?"

Will answered, "The original plan was tomorrow, but after last night's events, I think my wife will probably want to get the hell out of dodge as soon as possible."

Chief Patterson walked closer to Will and said, "I understand. Keeping the family safe is paramount. I'm planning to lift the shelter-in-place order in just a couple of hours. Something to keep in mind, there's a lot of wilderness between here and the main highway, a couple of hours' worth, and that's in good driving conditions. I suggest getting them on the road well before the evening. Safe travels to you."

All of the officers made their way into their vehicles and drove off the driveway and down the road.

Will made his way back into the house. Most of the family was still sleeping. *What a night!* Will thought. *I still can't wrap my mind around this. How do I explain this whole situation to the parents of Liam's friends? Explain the best I can I guess. The main objective is to get the family and those boys home safe to their families. Let the locals handle this situation. This isn't my fight. I'll just wait for Annie to wake up, and we'll figure out a game plan. We will probably need to stop back into town for supplies and fuel before we leave. I'll call ahead of time and see if the food store is even open considering the lockdown.*

A couple of hours later, an emergency text message was sent to Will's cell phone with an interesting alert tone. Will looked at his phone and read the message: "The emergency shelter-in-place order has been suspended for the remainder of the day. The Iron River Police Department will reactivate the shelter-in-place order one hour before dusk." By now, Will had started to make breakfast for the family and brew some more coffee for himself. He figured he'd start the day off right with a good breakfast with his family before they traveled home. The breakfast was complete with eggs, bacon, and biscuits with gravy. The wonderful smell of breakfast cooking slowly awoke the family as they made their way out of the bedrooms.

When Annie woke up she went over to her husband and gave him a long hug. Will said, "Figure it's best to get some fuel and supplies in town before we head home. Figure we leave here by the early afternoon."

Annie replied, "That sounds like a good plan. I would hate to leave my mom and dad here by themselves. They weren't planning to leave here until tomorrow. Tomorrow was their day to close up the house for the season."

Will replied, "Maybe we can convince the boys and even Boo to help your parents close up today before we leave. That way we all leave together."

Annie answered, "I think that will work. Let me run it past my parents after breakfast."

Eventually the whole family made their way through the kitchen. Even Robert and Ryan made healthy plates for themselves, and Ryan had seconds due to stress eating as he called it. Annie was busy talking for her folks. Liam could see from the commotion that things in and around the lake house were going to become a busy beehive of activity. Annie and Will assembled the family and the boys in the living room to hold a family meeting. As everyone came together, Annie began the speak, "Okay everyone, here's the deal. This morning we are going to help my parents clean this place top to bottom. After the house is clean, the kids will work together to take the dock out of the water as my parents cruise the boat back out to the launch and back into storage. Dad and I will be going into town to get fuel and supplies for our ride home. When everything is done and winterized for the season, we are planning to hit the road together. We plan to leave here by the early afternoon. Well before sunset. Any questions? Okay, let's get to work."

Everyone began to work together very smoothly. Tina was a very good delegator. As one kid finished a chore, she was ready to give them a new set of orders. Within a couple of hours, the house was clean enough for their liking. Annie and Will were getting ready to leave the house in their vehicle. Annie said, "We should be back soon, kids. Just do whatever the grandparents tell you so we can all get out of here." Soon enough Will and Annie were in their vehicle and on their way into town.

Liam, Ryan, Robert, and Boo were all outside helping the grandparents take out the dock. Before they finished the dock, Daniel and Tina boarded their boat. By then, the kids were getting the last of the dock secured to the shoreline. As Daniel drove, Tina said to us, "We will be back as soon as we can. You kids finish packing up your belongings. Grandpa and I have to take the boat out from the launch and drive it to the other property that has our winter shed. If you need anything call. Stay here and don't leave the property!" Tina and Daniel were now out of the shallow waters as Daniel began to fully open the motor. Within minutes, they were speeding toward the other side of the lake and out of sight.

As the group finished stacking the dock boards into a neat pile along the shoreline, Mike exited his patio door and walked toward the end of the deck. Mike seemed frustrated and enraged. Liam walked over to him and said, "How you holding up, Mike? How's the family?"

Mike replied in anger, "How do you think they're doing? My grandmother is beside herself. She hasn't got out of bed since the news. My mother is sitting in her room with the door closed trying to avoid the world."

Ryan came over. "And how's Rita?"

By then, Rita was making her way outside via the patio door. Mike answered, "Speak of the devil. Why don't you ask her yourself?"

Rita chimed into the conversation saying, "What are you losers up to?"

Liam answered, "We are helping our grandparents close up the lake house for the season. The plan is to leave here by early afternoon."

Mike replied, "Where are your parents and grandparents?"

Boo replied, "Mommy and Daddy are in town. Nana and Grandpa are taking the boat out of the water as we speak."

Mike was staring out toward the water and then looked back at his sister. Rita looked at Mike and said, "Mike, this isn't a good idea. Just forget it."

Mike interjected quickly, "We've already talked about this. If you're too scared stay here!"

Liam questioned, "What's going on?"

Rita answered, "Mike is going back to the wilderness. His plan is to find the native tribes and ask for their help to hunt down and kill the beast. I already told him to stay out of it!"

Mike shouted, "Shut up, Rita! This is our family! This is our fight! The police knew about this guy for years and didn't do anything about it because the old man was wealthy and kept this town afloat! Now I'm going out there with or without your help!"

Liam stepped into their argument. "Mike, if you made up your mind to go, you're not going there alone. I will come and help you."

Mike was silent for a moment as he thought about what Liam said. When he fell silent Ryan chimed into the conversation and said, "Damn it. I want to go home, but I can't leave my guy out here in the sticks by himself. I guess I'm in too!"

Then Robert entered into the conversation and said, "I agree. Can't leave my friends hanging. If I stick around here and wait for the grown-ups to return, I'll never be able to live this down back home. I'm in!"

Boo raised her hand and said, "I'm coming with too!"

Liam stared back at his sister and exclaimed, "Boo, you're too young. You stay here and wait for someone to come back!"

Boo replied, "Nope. That ain't happening. Your job is to watch me until Mommy and Daddy come back. Plus, if you leave me behind, my first move will be to call Mommy and Daddy on the phone. You wouldn't make it past Route 2!"

Liam answered, "Damn it! Fine! But you stay right next to me the entire time, okay?"

Rita shook her head in disapproval. "Mike, this is too dangerous. What can we, a group of kids, do against that thing?"

Mike nodded his head. "Okay. We all go and we have to go right now. Everyone just be cool and head to the jeep. I'll start her up, and we will make our way."

Ryan asked, "Dude, won't your mom or grandma hear us leaving?"

Mike answered as he chuckled, "Nope. Grandma doesn't have her hearing aids turned on, and my mom has her windows closed trying to block out the world right now. It would take the beast himself to knock in the front door to gain their attention."

Most of the crew made their way toward Mike's jeep. Ryan ran inside, gathered some food and water, and threw it into a picnic cooler. Liam made his way over to his grandfather's shed with his trail pack to gather a few supplies. Daniel was always an excellent Boy Scout. He kept the lake house well stocked with all kinds of supplies. Liam opened the door that led to the storage area and turned on the overhead light. As he looked around the room he thought, *Okay, what do we need? Let me see what we got. A Flashlight...Check! A couple of hacksaws....Check! A box of long matches....Check! Bug repellant....Check! Sledgehammer.... Check! And first-aid kit...Check! All right now we are in ready to roll!*

Liam put all of the supplies into his trail pack and walked briskly toward Mike's jeep. Ryan was already loading the cooler into the back of the jeep as Liam climbed aboard. The jeep was a bit overfull now with Boo riding along, so she sat on Liam's lap. Mike started the jeep. Rita was riding shotgun. She turned to Mike and asked, "How do you expect to roll out of town unobserved, Mike? There's police everywhere."

Mike replied, "As quickly and as carefully as I can. Everyone just be cool. I got this!"

CHAPTER 33

....

MEETING CHIEF BIG BEAR TOE'S SON

The group made their way gingerly along the side road that emptied into Sunset Valley Lake Road. They turned onto the main road that led to Route 2, and Mike opened up the throttle. They were speeding down the road when Rita exclaimed, "Mike, slow down. Cops ahead!"

They were approaching the Schubert family estate. A couple of state police cars were parked in the driveway. To their luck, none of the members from either the state police or its forensic team were outside the house. Liam assumed as they rolled past the estate that the team was probably busy sorting through whatever evidence inside the house. As the road turned and they made their way out of sight, Mike again increased his speed at they headed toward Route 2.

They reached Route 2 and were surprised by the amount of activity on the road. There were several trucks with their trailers rolling down the road toward town. Other trucks carried boats attached to their trailer hitches. They turned west on Route 2 toward downtown Iron River and passed up the main local supermarket. Boo and Liam tucked down a bit as they saw their parents' vehicle in the parking lot. The vehicle was empty. Mike looked back at Liam and Boo and said, "I don't think you have to worry. Looks like half the town is in the supermarket right now. Your parents are probably stuck in long lines at the checkout."

Boo and Liam were both relieved their parents weren't in the parking lot loading the van as they drove past. They rolled toward downtown Main Street. There was a line of cars and trucks waiting to enter the two gas stations in town. Ryan said, "What do you make of all of this, Mike?"

Mike replied, "Looks like everyone has the same idea as your folks. They're all packing up and hitting the road before nightfall!"

The number of people and their vehicles worked toward the group's advantage. They didn't have to act like they were running away or hiding from the police. The police were cruising up and down the streets, and some officers were parked outside the grocery store and gas stations to help with traffic control.

As they passed up the library and the church where they sheltered in place the previous evening, they were getting closer to the town limits. Mike looked back at everyone and said, "Looks like we are in the clear. No roadblocks or checkpoints ahead. A couple of blocks to go!"

They were stopped at the intersection where the gruesome scene unfolded the night before. Mike grew impatient by the red light, but he kept his cool, even though they saw a state trooper rolling down the intersecting street toward them. The light turned yellow and then red for the state trooper as he arrived at the intersection. The group could tell that the trooper was looking at them. Mike whispered, "Just remain cool and just smile and nod. Everything will be fine."

The light turned green, and they made their way through the intersection and out of town. Liam tried not to look back, but he couldn't help himself. He saw the light turn and then state trooper made his way through the intersection slowly as he watched the jeep travel out of town. Liam was waiting for the trooper to turn on the lights and turn sharply toward their direction of travel. To their fortune, the trooper kept driving down the road away from them. Liam felt a sigh of relief but also dread to what lies ahead in the wilderness.

The group marched on, and it was early afternoon as they passed through the town of Watersmeet. Liam figured by now his folks should be home and probably wondering where they were. As Liam thought this, his phone began to light up. It was his dad! Liam knew he was in trouble without even hitting the talk button. He didn't answer, and it went to voice mail. He turned off his phone. Moments later, Rita looked at her phone. It was her mother! Rita said, "Oh crap. It's Mom. I think our secret is out, Mike. The grown-ups are looking for us!"

Mike replied, "We are already driving through Watersmeet and we will be entering the wilderness within the hour. Even if they head this way, we have a decent head start! Rita, take a look at that map printout again. Try to find some landmarks that can help us find the native tribes."

Rita searched the map intensely. After a few moments, Rita said, "If my map reading is correct, I think their main settlement grounds are a couple of miles northwest of Lake Gogebic. That's an area between their fishing grounds along the lake and the other main fishing grounds along Lake Superior. According to this map, there should be a small road from the split in the main road that will lead from the northwest section of the lake to their main settlement. That's the road we didn't travel down yesterday. But I can't see where the road ends."

Robert looked on his phone and said, "I only have one bar now. We will probably lose reception soon. I don't see another road on the map on my phone. Are you sure it's there?"

Mike replied, "Unless...of course! It's probably past that road that was gated off. Remember the one we saw!"

Rita looked at the map again and said, "That would make sense. That's the only other road that we came across in that area."

They approached the wilderness as they did previously. Mike drove the jeep as far down the road as he could, farther than he drove previously. They finally reached the end of the road that was gated off with that familiar sign: "No Trespassing Beyond This Point, Hazardous Area, Abandoned Mine Shafts." They all exited the jeep and walked toward the gate. The gate stretched from one side of the road to the other. The road was surrounded by heavy brush and timber, too much for even the jeep to navigate through. The fence swung inward toward the forbidden area. It was secured by a heavy lock and chain in the middle separating the two sides of the fence posts.

Mike looked at the heavy lock and said, "Hey, Ryan, if you're hungry why don't you chew on this lock for a bit and see if it opens."

Ryan said, "Screw you, Mike! I'm not that hungry, but I am growing hangry. I'm getting some of that trail mix that's in the cooler."

As Ryan walked toward the jeep Liam said, "Hey, Ryan, while you're over there, bring over my trail pack!"

Ryan picked up the trail pack and exclaimed, "Good Lord, Liam. This thing weighs a ton. What do you have inside of this thing?"

Liam answered, "Bring it over and I'll show you!"

Ryan bought the pack over and Liam opened it.

Robert looked into the bag, chuckled, and said, "You always were the best Boy Scout. Always prepared."

Liam pulled out the sledgehammer and handed it to Mike and said, "You're the strongest of us. If you hit it right, this will be our key to getting inside."

Mike grabbed ahold of the sledgehammer and walked over to the lock. He took a couple of big swings. Within three or four hard knocks, the lock broke and the chain fell to the ground!

Mike smiled at his handy work and said, "Good job, Liam. Looks like your key worked. Everyone back into the jeep!"

They all did what Mike asked. He handed the sledgehammer back over to Liam and then opened the gates on both sides. They were now driving down the forbidden territory. They drove along the road for about a mile when they came across an old building. The building looked abandoned. It was old masonry building. It looked something like the old warehouses in and around Chicago. The building was roughly 100 feet long, and it was wide and stood two stories with large old windows boarded up from the outside. Mike slowed down the jeep as everyone looked at this massive building that seemed out of place in the middle of nowhere. Liam asked Mike, "What do you make of this, Mike?"

Mike shook his head as he looked at the building and said, "I'm not sure. Looks old and you can tell that it hasn't been used in years. My best guess is it was used during the old mining days. Maybe some kind of factory and gathering area for the raw materials."

Ryan chimed in, "Looks like you can still access the building by the front door. That's the only way in or out that isn't boarding up. Anyone want to go in and check it out?"

Mike answered, "Sure, big guy. I'll be right after you."

Ryan replied, "Nope. No thanks. I'm good without going in. Curiosity killed the cat. Let's not repeat history."

The road continued past the building and over the hills toward the abandoned mines. In the distance they could see smokestacks. Boo looked up and said, "Look! That's probably the settlement just beyond those hills!"

Mike looked down at Boo and said, "I think you're right. That's our next stop."

Mike drove toward the smokestacks in the distance.

They passed some of the entrances of the old mines. Each entrance was boarded up with a wooden X and a sign reading: "No Trespassing, Dangerous Area, Keep Out!" The road took them through the mining area and over the hills. As they reached the top of the hill, they were greeted by two men on horseback. Each of whom were armed with rifle along the side of their harness. One of the men extended his hand out to signify stop while the other man exclaimed, "Halt! Stop right there!" Mike did as he instructed and stopped the jeep. The two men came alongside both the passenger's and driver's sides of the jeep. They could tell the group was surprised and nervous by their imitating presence. Both men were of middle-aged years. They both had long dark hair and features. The clothes resembled something similar to what others would recognize as Native American. Liam said to Mike, "I think we met who we've been looking for, Mike."

Mike replied, "Just be cool, everyone."

The man on the driver's side of the jeep looked down at Mike saying, "What are you kids doing here on our land? This land is part of our reservation. The only outsiders welcome here are those who are welcomed by our chief."

Liam replied nervously, "Chief Big Bear Toe?"

The man on the passenger's side asked, "How do you know about Chief Big Bear Toe, young man?"

Liam answered, "I saw his paintings in an old antique shop that's owned by Mr. Nick Rosalie. And we did some research on this history of the area at the Iron River Library."

One of the men answered, "Interesting. What brings you out this far away from your homes?"

Mike answered, "It's my fault, sir. I came out here because the beast killed my grandfather. It seems like the police chief and some old lady in town knew about this beast for a long time. And from our research your tribe battled this beast before. I came out here looking for help. My sister and my new friends here came along with me so I wasn't alone."

The man at the driver's side door said, "That's very brave of you young people to venture out here with your friend. Why risk it?" He looked down at Liam and said, "I have a feeling each of you has seen the beast for yourselves. Is that true?"

They all nodded their heads. Liam replied, "Yes, sir. That's correct. We were out here last night. It followed us back home. The town was under siege by the beast, and a couple of police officers were killed."

The man at the passenger's side door replied, "The day grows short. Forgive me for not introducing myself. My name is Little Feather. This is my brother Eagle's Wing. We will take you to our chief. He will know what's best."

Liam asked, "Mr. Rosalie said Chief Big Bear Toe passed away. Is that true?"

Eagle's Wing answered, "Yes this is true. He was a true leader and warrior. His son, Little Bear Toe, is now our chief. We will bring you to him. Follow us!"

Mike did as he was instructed. He followed the two men on their horses through the main tribe settlement. They passed by several men who were surprised by their presence. It was like they entered an entirely different world. The entire campsite was surrounded by flowers that were similar to the wolf's-bane that was outside the church and Sunset Valley Lake properties. The men instructed Mike to park the jeep just alongside one of the main huts.

As they exited the jeep, Eagle's Wing said, "Wait here as we talk to our chief."

The men walked into the hut as the group waiting with uneasy patience. They could overhear some of the conversation inside the hut. They weren't able to gather what was being discussed since they were speaking in their native language. At first, the conversation seemed heated, but after Little Feather and Eagle's Wing explained the situation, the chief seemed to have calmed down. After several uneasy minutes, Little Feather exited the hut and said, "Come in all of you, and welcome. The chief will see you now."

CHAPTER 34

....

WE HAVE TO GET
TO THOSE KIDS!

They all entered the hut where the chief was sitting on the ground. There was a small fire in the middle of the hut. Smoke exited along the center opening in the canopy. The space was filled with scattered items that were placed in an orderly fashion. One section had a sleeping area. Another was a place for his weapons and hunting tools. Along the walls resting on the floor were some of the paintings that were like the ones Liam saw in Mr. Rosalie's antique shop. The chief looked at the group and said, "Please, all of you. Sit and be welcomed to our land and our home." They all did as the chief instructed. He continued to speak. "I am Little Bear Toe. Son of the late Big Bear Toe. I am the chief of my people. Little Feather and Eagle's Wing informed me of your situation. I'm sorry to hear of you grandfather, young man. Tell me about him and why you are here."

Mike began. "Thank you, Chief, for granting us your time. I know that my grandfather was killed by the beast."

Chief Little Bear Toe interjected and said, "You mean the werewolf!"

Mike replied respectfully, "Yes, sir! The werewolf. We were in this area last night. It followed us home and attacked the town!"

Liam chimed into the conversation and said, "And, Chief. It seems like the chief of Iron River Police knows a lot about the werewolf and kept it secret for years."

Chief Little Bear Toe answered, "You're correct, young man. I was a boy when it happened. My father along with several of our hunters accompanied Chief Patterson, Mr. Rosalie, Mr. Schubert, and his brother on a hunting mission to kill the wolf years ago. That's one of the reasons the old mines closed close to here. A couple of miners were attacked and killed by the werewolf while they were working late into the evening. Along with several other attacks, it forced the hand of our tribe and the local people of Iron River."

Liam asked the chief, "So, what happened during this hunting party? And how long have you known about the werewolf?"

The chief answered, "Very good questions, young man. First, we don't know exactly when the curse of the werewolf started. Legend tells of a story that an elder tribal hunter from one of the other native tribes that used to live in this area. The story that has been passed down for generations says this hunter was on a hunt for extra meat during the fall months. They would often hunt during the full moons when the prey were more active and easier to spot with the glow of the moon. They were hunting deer and bear when their hunting group was attacked by a huge alpha wolf and his pack. Several hunters were killed, but one of the hunters killed the alpha wolf. But before the alpha died it severely wounded this hunter, and that was the beginning of the curse. My father tried several times to track and hunt this werewolf but was unsuccessful. Until he joined forces with the men from Iron River. They met the beast on this hunting ground during the orange glow of the October moon when the beast was at his height of strength and hunger. My father always believed that this was the animal instinct to feed in preparation for the winter months ahead. This orange moon will rise into the night's sky tonight. This is the night my people dread the most. In your culture you celebrate Halloween. In our culture we prepare for this night with uneasy eagerness."

The chief took a brief pause and continued answering. "When the men from Iron River joined forces with my father they battled the werewolf. Unfortunately, many men were killed, along with Mr. Schubert's brother. To my understanding, Mr. Schubert was the man who laid the killing blow to the wolf, but he, too, was wounded by the wolf before it died. And so the curse was passed down to him. Chief Patterson knew about this, but Mr. Schubert reassured him he would be able to control it. My father told me he learned from Chief Patterson that Mr. Schubert formed a strategy in order to tackle the beast within. On the night of the half-moon, Mr. Schubert would barricade himself in his house in order to cage the beast. But on nights of the full and new moon, he was worried that his power would be too strong and he would escape from the prison he made in his house. On those days, he would make his way out to that old abandoned mining building and lock himself inside of it. The goal was to be as far away from his town as possible. We have taken our precautions on those nights. We move the women and children to the far western coast along our fishing settlement. Both of our settlements are surrounded by wolf's-bane. Our hunters take watch over the settlement throughout the night. For years he and the beast within have been able to stay locked in that building all night without incident."

Mike said to the chief, "That's the problem, Chief. We believe that Mr. Schubert is starting to lose control over the beast within as he has gotten older. Last night during the full moon, the wolf was outside the building and going on a rampage all the way back in Iron River."

Chief Little Bear Toe looked at everyone and seemed shocked by this news. He stood up and asked Eagle's Wing over to his side. In his native language he said something to Eagle's Wing that sent him running outside the hut. Ryan asked, "What did you tell Eagle's Wing, Chief?"

The chief answered, "My men and I thought we heard the howls of the werewolf outside the building last night. We attempted to search, but it was not to be found. I told him to gather the men and prepare them for battle, for tonight we hunt!"

Rita stood up in surprise and said, "What do you mean, Chief?"

The chief answered, "Tonight is the night my warriors have been preparing for a generation. We knew that the possibility was there that one day that old man wouldn't be able to control the beast. We end this tonight!"

The chief walked over to the entrance of his hut and observed his men gathering their weapons and preparing for battle. He then looked at the setting sun. "These days in the fall grow short, and the time for the werewolf is near. It's too far to get you to the lands where we take our women and children for safety. You must stay here with us. We will protect you. But you must also be armed with weapons in order to protect yourselves!"

Liam looked at Boo as she grabbed ahold of him. She was scared and started to cry. Liam looked down at Boo and said, "Don't worry, Boo. Everything will be okay. I'm your big brother. I'll protect you!"

✦ ✦ ✦

Meanwhile, back in Iron River, Daniel, Tina, Will, Annie, Gabby, and Rita and Mike's mom, Jennea, were frantically trying to call their kids with no answer. Annie was furious exclaiming, "Where the hell can they be? When was the last time you saw them, Mom?"

Tina answered, "The last time we saw them we were on the boat heading toward the boat launch! Your father and I were gone for about an hour. They must have left the property during that time. I told them to stay on the property!"

Will chimed in, "The timeline makes sense, Annie. The lines were super long at the grocery store and the gas station. We were gone for over an hour ourselves. We didn't mean to take so long, but it could be helped!"

Gabby asked Will, "Where do you think they went?"

Will answered, "I'm afraid of the answer. I think they might have made their way into town or maybe out toward the wilderness again."

Jennea looked at Annie and Will and said, "Oh my God! What do we do? The day is marching on, and it will be evening soon!"

Will looked at everyone and said, "Okay here's the plan. Mom, Dad, you stay here just in case they come back. Jennea, you come with us. Gabby, you stay with my parents. If the kids make it home, call us right away. Dad, do you still have your old hunting rifle on the property?"

Daniel answered, "Yes, it's in the safe."

Will replied, "Grab it for me please; I'll be back in a minute."

Annie ran after Will and said, "Will, honey, what are you planning to do? This is crazy!"

Will walked over to the storage shed and grabbed his old fire axe he kept on the property to chop wood and said, "We have to go and get our kids, Annie. And we will do it by any means necessary!"

Annie asked Will, "Where are we going?"

Will answered, "First stop is to the police station to talk to Chief Patterson. Maybe someone saw the kids while they were on patrol. If they haven't, I'll ask for his help."

Daniel had retrieved his hunting rifle, handed it to Will, and said, "Be careful, Son!"

Will replied, "Thanks, Dad. I'll get those kids home. Nothing will happen to anyone. I promise! And if Chief Patterson doesn't help, I'll ask him for some of those silver bullets he keeps in this trunk. We have to get those kids. Jennea, Annie, get in the car. We are leaving!"

As Will, Annie, and Jennea heading toward the police station, Chief Patterson was already there talking to Nick Rosalie. Nick asked Chief Patterson, "Have we found anything, Rich?"

Chief Patterson answered, "Nothing yet. Well, besides the horror show at the Schubert estate. We haven't found old man Schubert. He could be anywhere! You know it's the new moon tonight, right?"

Nick answered, "No! I thought that wasn't for a couple of days!"

Chief Patterson replied, "He's probably out in the wilderness, Nick. He's probably hiding out in that old abandoned building near the old mine shafts right now as we speak, just waiting for the moon to rise. Let's end this tonight!"

Mr. Rosalie nodded his head in approval.

Chief Patterson called over Chief Wellington and said, "Chief, come over here if you would!"

Chief Wellington was having coffee and a donut at the watch desk. He walked over to Chief Patterson and asked, "What do you need, Rich?"

Chief Patterson said, "You up for a hunt, old friend?"

Chief Wellington answered, "When do we leave?"

Chief Patterson said, "In a few minutes; we'll take my car."

During this time, one of the state troopers was walking into the police station after an afternoon on patrol. Chief Patterson asked the trooper, "How's everything going, son? Anything to report?"

The trooper answered, "Nothing much, Chief. Just a lot of people getting in and out of town throughout the day. Helped with traffic control for a bit. There's one thing that was bugging me though."

Chief Patterson asked, "What's that, son?"

The trooper answered, "I was on my way to the gas station to help with traffic control. I saw a group of kids heading west along Route 2. They looked kind of young. Figured maybe they were heading toward Watersmeet."

Nick exclaimed, "What type of car was it?"

The trooper answered, "A jeep. It was filled with kids."

Nick and Chief Patterson looked at each other. Chief Patterson said, "Thank you for the report, son. Stay here at the watch desk and help answer the phones. Mr. Rosalie and Chief Wellington are coming with me to investigate something."

Nick, Chief Patterson, and Chief Wellington made a quick walk outside and into Chief Patterson's squad car. Nick said to the chiefs, "Damn it. Those kids are heading back to the wilderness!"

Chief Patterson replied, "Sounds about right. Buckle up, boys. We are going out west!"

Chief Patterson turned the ignition, quickly back up his squad car, turned on the lights and sirens, and accelerated quickly away from the police station and onto Route 2 toward the wilderness.

CHAPTER 35

....

THE NEW MOON RISES

The sun was beginning to set over the hills in the wilderness region. The group were waiting in the chief's hut as the men prepared for battle. A great fire was set in the middle of the settlement. The warriors sang songs in their native language. They loaded their weapons and drew face paint on each other's faces. The chief was looking through a small mirror as he applied face paint to himself. In total there were five men preparing for battle. Eagle's Wing came into the hut and said, "Chief, the men are ready."

Liam asked Eagle's Wing, "What are the names of the other two men in the hunting party?"

Eagle's Wing pointed toward the two other men and answered, "The smaller one over there is my brother. His name is Little Red-Eyed Loon. He's the youngest of us, but he's still an excellent hunter. The bigger one is Evening Hawk. He's the oldest and most experienced hunter in our tribe. He helped train me and Little Feather when we were young boys."

The chief gathered his rifle and his spear, walked toward Eagle's Wing, and looked down at the group. The chief said, "All of you come and walk with me."

They all walked outside with the chief.

Rita asked, "Where are we going?"

The chief answered, "Over here to our weapons hut. You will need something to protect yourselves."

When the chief said those words, they were all instantly nervous. Robert asked, "What do you mean, Chief? You don't expect us to go on the hunt with you?"

163

Chief Little Bear Toe answered, "Of course not, young man." The chief walked into the hut and said, "Stay outside here." After a few moments, the chief exited the hut with several small piercing weapons. He said, "Here. Each of you will be armed with one of these hunting knives. They are each made of pure silver. And for the older one I give you this spear. This spear has been in our tribe for generations. It's heavy and reliable. The tip of the blade is pure silver. Everyone gather around!"

Each of the men gathered around the group and the chief. They were all armed with rifles and piercing weapons along with long torches. The chief came up to each one of the men and blessed them over their foreheads. After the blessing, they mounted their horses and each man went over to the large fires and lit their torches. The chief spoke to all everyone, "Men, it's now time to test our skills and claim our rights as warriors of our tribe! Little Feather, Eagle's Wing, and Evening Hawk, you ride with me. We ride toward the abandoned building and hunt the werewolf until the end. Little Red-Eyed Loon, you are the youngest of party. You must stay here as a last line of defense and protect the young people."

Little Red-Eye Loon seamed disappointed by this news and said, "Chief, I am ready for battle. I must—"

The chief interjected and said, "You must do what I've instructed. You have a very important mission. Light the torches around the camp and protect these young people at all costs!"

✦ ✦ ✦

Meanwhile, back in Iron River, Will, Annie, and Jennea parked outside the police station and quickly ran inside. They walked right over to the front desk where the state trooper was sitting. The trooper asked, "How can I help you folks?"

Will answered, "We need to talk to Chief Patterson right away. It's about our kids!"

The trooper replied, "Sorry folks, the chief isn't here. They left with Chief Wellington and some other gentleman some time ago."

Annie exclaimed, "He left! Where did he go?"

The trooper, growing a bit impatient by the line of questions, said, "Folks! Listen, he isn't here. All I know he left rather quickly after I told him about the groups of kids I saw heading out of town."

Jennea asked frantically, "Some kids were leaving town! What kind of vehicle were they driving?"

The trooper answered, "It was a jeep heading westbound along Route 2 toward Watersmeet. Were they your kids?"

Will answered, "Yes! They are supposed to be heading home with us!"

The trooper asked, "Were those the kids from last night?"

Annie answered, "Yes, sir! We believe they might be heading back to the wilderness as we speak!"

The trooper answered, "It's going to be evening soon, and the chief's shelter-in-place order will be in effect. I got kids of my own too. I'll try to reach the chief on the radio."

The trooper walked over to the radio and said, "State police from Iron River HQ to Iron River Command." He repeated the message a few times with no answer. He walked back over to the concerned parents and said, "I couldn't get him on the radio. That's never good. That could mean he's in trouble. I can only imagine what you folks are going through. Tell you what. Meet me outside and follow me in my cruiser." The trooper walked over to one of his fellow troopers as Will, Annie, and Jennea headed to their vehicle.

Just then, Bobby pulled up in his squad car. Bobby exited his car and said, "Heard the commotion on my scanner at home. I had to come in. What's going on, Will?"

Will answered, "It's our kids, Bobby! They left town and we believe they are heading out to the wilderness!"

Within a minute, the trooper and Bobby ran over to one of the squad cars. The trooper signaled for Will to follow him. With lights and sirens, Will followed the police escort out of the town limits and toward the wilderness.

✦✦✦

The chief watched as the sun was now having its last moments before complete sunset. They said a prayer out load toward the sun. Each warrior fell silent and prayed with the chief. The group were in complete disbelief of what was happening around them. After the chief completed his prayer, Little Feather, Eagle's Wing, Evening Hawk, and the chief started to ride quickly toward the abandoned building. The moon was now starting to rise over the hills. The hunt was on! Little Red-Eyed Loon did as he was instructed. He rode his horse over to each of the torches that were positioned above the ground along the permitter of the camp. Mike walked over to him and asked, "Anything we can do to help you, sir?"

Little Red-Eyed Loon looked at Mike and said, "No, young man. The best thing you can do is stay together near the chief hut. I'll be guarding the perimeter throughout the night."

They all did as he instructed. Rita curled up next to her brother. Boo was no more than an arm's reach from Liam. Ryan looked at Robert and said, "I'm scared but I ain't holding you, bro."

Robert chuckled a bit and said, "Of course you would say something like that. If I was holding a big beef sandwich, I bet you would be inching close to me asking for a bite."

Ryan laughed and said, "So you're the horror movie expert. What are the odds that me make it back to Chicago safe and sound?"

Robert answered, "Considering this isn't some movie and this is real, I'll give us a 50/50 shot."

Ryan replied, "That's all! Wow! But if we make it out of here, it will be a pretty cool story. Maybe good enough to get you a girlfriend, bro."

Robert and Ryan both laughed. Robert said, "I should be scared and curled up in a ball right now, but I'm not. I feel safe around my friends. Especially you, big guy."

CHAPTER 36

....

THE ABANDONED BUILDING

Chief Little Bear Toe, Eagle's Wing, Little Feather, and Evening Hawk made their way to the abandoned building as the new moon was now rising. They each threw their torches to the ground and dismounted their horses. They placed the piercing end of their torches into the ground as they walked around the perimeter of the building. There wasn't any movement around the building nor were there any sounds coming from inside. Chief Little Bear Toe gave out orders and said, "Eagle's Wing and Little Feather on me. We are going inside. Evening Hawk, stay outside and guard the perimeter. Signal for us if needed."

Little Feather was the first to approach the front door and said, "Chief, I don't think the wolf is inside. The door isn't locked."

Chief Little Bear Toe was baffled by this revelation and said, "Let's go inside and clear the building before we expand outward."

All three men entered the building with their rifles drawn and ready for fire.

They were immediately greeted by the horrific smell from inside the building. It smelled like wild animals and rotting animal flesh. The smell was so bad it caused Little Feather to start gaging into a corner. The chief turned on the flashlight that he carried on a sling along his waist. It illuminated the carnage around them as he shined the light from one side of the large building to another. Around them were the remains of several large dead animals. Most of them wild deer and turkeys. They continued to scan the large open area, being mindful not to slip and fall onto the carnage at their feet. Eagle's Wing also shined his flashlight and shouted out loud, "Chief. Oh my God look at this!"

Chief Big Bear Toe went toward Eagle's Wing to find out what frightened him. As he approached Eagle's Wing, he saw a pile of human skeletons that were stacked in a corner! The chief exclaimed, "On the souls of my ancestors, what the hell is all of this?"

Eagle's Wing answered, "Looks like that old man has been disposing of his mistakes in this old building for a long time, Chief. A lot of fisherman, campers, hikers, and hunters have all vanished over the years. This would explain their disappearance!"

As the chief examined the remains scattered in a corner pile, there was a sudden load howl. The chief exclaimed, "Sounds like it's just outside the building!"

Just then, there was a horrible loud scream. It was Evening Hawk!

The chief shouted, "That's Evening Hawk! Come on!"

They ran outside only to find it was too late. Evening Hawk, the best among them, was killed and lying on the ground!

Little Feather exclaimed, "He didn't even get a shot off!"

Chief Little Bear Toe ordered, "Eyes up, all of you. Spread out! He's here!"

They searched around the compound and couldn't find anything.

All of the remaining men searched the immediate area and then gathered together next to the entrance of the building. Eagle's Wing exclaimed, "Where the hell did it go!"

Just then Little Feather felt something fall on his head. It was blood! All of them looked up and saw the two yellow eyes of the werewolf staring down at them!

The chief exclaimed, "Oh my God! Fire! Fire! Fire!"

They quickly raised their guns, but it was too late. The beast quickly fell from the roof and landed on Little Feather and Eagle's Wing! Both were killed instantly from the razor-sharp claws of the beast! The impact was so great it threw Chief Little Bear Toe to the ground, knocking his rifle several feet away from him. The werewolf took its time feeding off the two fallen warriors as the chief stumbled to his feet and ran toward his weapon. As the chief came close to his weapon, the wolf looked at the chief, growled, and let out a loud howl. The werewolf ran as quick as lightning toward the chief! The chief fired his weapon and hit the beast in its arm. It wasn't a killing hit, but it was enough to stun the beast for a few moments.

The chief quickly mounted his horse and headed back toward the camp. He figured the only defense he had was Little Red-Eyed Loon and the wolf's-bane that surrounded the camp. As he rode his horse, he looked back only to see the beast beginning to chase him. His wounding shot was enough to slow him down for the chief to make it close to camp.

Little Red-Eyed Loon continued his duties at the camp. Walking the perimeter and keeping sharp eye on the young people. As he completed another perimeter sweep, he saw the chief riding at full speed toward the camp. He galloped with his horse toward the chief and asked, "What's happening, Chief?"

The chief exclaimed as loudly as he could, "It's here! It's here! Be ready. It took out Little Feather and—"

Just then, the werewolf came out of the chief's blindside and knocked him off of his horse, sending him flying into the darkness outside the perimeter. Little Red-Eyed Loon tried to see where the chief and the werewolf were located. All he could hear was the beast dragging the chief into the darkness of the wilderness as the chief let out cries of terror!

The group ran toward Little Red-Eyed Loon. Mike exclaimed, "What happened? What's going on? What happened to the chief and the other men?"

Red Eyed Loon answered, "I don't know! Just stay over near the chief hut!"

Just then, there was the horrific scream and then complete silence as the werewolf took a final fatal blow to Chief Little Bear Toe. There was nothing but complete silence for several minutes as Little Red-Eyed Loon tried to find the beast while staying inside the perimeter. The silence was broken by the sound of sirens and the sight of flashing lights approaching from the other side of the perimeter. It was Chief Patterson's car.

All of the men exited the vehicle and ran toward the kids. Little Red-Eyed Loon rode his horse toward the men at maximum speed. Chief Patterson, Chief Wellington, and Nick Rosalie all ran up to the group as they were relieved by their presence. Liam gave Nick Rosalie a hug and said, "God, I'm so happy you are here, Mr. Rosalie! How did you find us?"

Nick answered, "I'm glad I'm here too, kid. Chief Patterson knew about this location for some time."

Little Red-Eyed Loon began to tell them the situation. "Men, the werewolf is here and we are—"

Suddenly, the body of Chief Little Bear Toe was thrown into the camp, knocking over one of torches. The torch lit the ground and the wolf's-bane protecting the perimeter.

Little by little, the flames overtook the camp, engulfing the protection of the wolf's-bane that kept the group safe. Little Red-Eyed Loon, Chief Patterson, Chief Wellington, and Nick Rosalie surrounded and protected the kids with their weapons as they gazed at the werewolf on the other side of the flames. The beast stared at them with his two yellow eyes. Blood was dripping down from its disgusting mouth. His teeth were grinding as he continued to flex his razor-sharp claws. The beast was clever enough to continue moving quickly in and out of the darkness behind the flames in order to not allow a clean shot. Rita screamed, "Good God! Why isn't he attacking?"

Nick Rosalie answered, "The werewolf is like any other creature. It's terrified of fire! We have to think of something quick! What about hightailing it back to the squad car!"

Chief Patterson thought for a moment and said, "Won't do any good. I wouldn't be able to put it in drive before that bastard was on top of us!" Chief Patterson looked over to Chief Wellington and Little Red-Eyed Loon and then looked back Nick Rosalie. He ordered, "Chief Wellington, and you, sir,"—he looked at Little Red-Eyed Loon—"when the fire dies down, we will stay here and hold our ground and protect the kids. Nick, take the kids back to the old mines. Wait there until we get there or the sun comes up!"

Nick replied, "No way, Chief! I ain't leaving this fight. I'm finishing it!"

Chief Patterson said, "You may have to, Nick! Enter the old iron mine shaft! It leads to the silver mines. That may be our last line of defense!"

The flames started to die down. The werewolf continued to run back and forth around the perimeter until he could find a clearing.

It circled around until it reached Chief Patterson's squad car. The beast took his razor-sharp claws and punctured a couple of the tires. Chief Wellington said, "Damn it, there goes plan C. I was hoping to get the heck out of here if all else fails!"

Chief Patterson looked back toward the trail that led to the mines and said, "Nick, it's now or never. Take the kids and protect them as best as you can. We'll cover you. Go!"

Nick agreed and said, "Goodbye, old friend. All right, kids, on me! Let's move!"

The group quickly grabbed their weapons. Liam also grabbed his trail pack and tossed it over his shoulder. Little Red-Eyed Loon, Chief Patterson, and Chief Wellington were in front of the group. Nick and the kids ran behind them. The beast encircled the area in front of the men as the they waited to engage their target. The beast tried to follow after the group, but they were fortunate to still have flames covering their escape to the mines. The men ran toward the beast, trying to get a shot and waiting for it to charge their position. The group ran as quickly as they could.

Mike and Rita were the first ones to enter the mines. Boo, Robert, Ryan, and Liam followed soon after. The last one to enter the mines was Mr. Rosalie. Nick took one last look at the men protecting their escape. They looked scared but determined to kill the beast and protect the kids by any means necessary. Nick entered the mine.

Rita said, "How are we supposed to see anything down here? I can't see a foot in front of my face!"

Nick Rosalie searched his pockets. "I must have dropped my flashlight. I should have my lighter. Damn it! I left it in the chief's car!"

Liam opened his trail pack. He took out his flashlight. But before they left the house, he didn't check the batteries. The light was starting to fade; the batteries had almost no energy left. Liam took out his matches, a roll of bandage wrap, the alcohol first-aid prep, and the hacksaws. Ryan turned to Liam, looked down, and said, "What are you doing, Mr. Boy Scout?"

Liam turned to him and said, "Just hold my flashlight before we run out of juice. I'm making some torches." Liam wrapped some bandage wrap around the working end of the hacksaws, dripped some alcohol over the cloth, and lit the bandage with a couple of his matches.

Nick Rosalie said, "Good thinking, kid. You remind me of me! Let me get ahold of those things so you can get to your feet. I'll lead the way!"

CHAPTER 37

....

THE SILVER MINES

The fire was decaying now. The layers of protection that surrounded the camp were now gone. The men outside the mines spread out in order to properly defend the wide unprotected area in front of them. Little Red-Eyed Loon looked at Chief Patterson and said, "What's the plan, sir?"

Chief Patterson said, "The only way into the mines is right behind us. Just protect the opening and try to kill this bastard!"

Chief Wellington said, "Keep it simple. Always like it simple, Rich."

They could hear the werewolf in the darkness surrounding the camp. Chief Patterson said, "Anyone see him?"

Little Red-Eyed Loon said, "No, sir. He keeps moving, changing his position. I guarantee you it can see us!" Little Red-Eyed Loon was on point as Chief Patterson and Chief Wellington covered the flank around him. All of the men had their guns at the ready, waiting for that killing strike! Little Red-Eyed Loon moved forward, thinking he could hear the werewolf just a few yards in front of his vision.

Chief Patterson noticed Little Red-Eyed Loon moving forward. He shouted, "Son! I would stay close to us if I were—"

Just then, the beast ran quickly toward Little Red-Eyed Loon from his blindside! Little Red-Eyed Loon tried to turn in time, but it was too late. The beast sent him flying into the air! His rifle fell several feet away from him. Little Red-Eyed Loon scrambled to pull out his silver knife from his side pouch as his last line of defense. He struggled to remove the safety clip around the knife. He could hear the growl of the beast over him. Little Red-Eyed Loon looked up and started to gag over the monster's breath as he let out a horrible scream. The werewolf injected his teeth into Little Red-Eyed Loon's neck! Within seconds, the screams fell silent.

"Son! Young man! Are you there?" Chief Patterson exclaimed.

Chief Wellington replied, "He's gone, Rich! Just you and me. Let's kill this bastard!"

Both chiefs moved forward. Chief Patterson told Chief Wellington, "Cover my six! Let's bring the fight to him!" Chief Patterson stared out into the darkness unable to locate the beast. He shouted, "Old man, Schubert! You can't fight against this thing anymore! If you have any type of control left, just step forward enough so I can see you! I promise I will end it quickly. This will all be over! There's no going back home after tonight!"

From out of the darkness there was a howl so loud the group could hear it echoing into the chambers of the mines. The werewolf began to charge quickly toward Chief Patterson! Chief Patterson lined up his shot and fired. The beast dodges the first bullet. The beast moved faster and closer. Chief Patterson exclaimed, "This is the end you old—"

Chief Patterson attempted to fire his weapon, but the rifle jammed! The monster lunged forward and laid his blood-stained claws into Chief Patterson, piercing his bullet-proof vest.

Chief Wellington turned to check on his friend and hopefully fire his weapon. As he turned, the werewolf was right behind him! The beast grabbed ahold of his rifle. Chief Wellington fired, but the bullet went flying off into the walls of the mine. The beast plunged his claws into the right leg of Chief Wellington, making him collapse. He looked up at the beast as it towered over him. There was another loud scream that could be heard throughout the chambers of the mines. All they heard after was a faint "Run!" and then silence.

Nick Rosalie stopped for a second and turned toward the sounds of his friends. He knew it was too late. He looked back at the group and said, "Let's keep going; it's not too far."

Rita frantically asked Mr. Rosalie, "Where the hell are we going?"

Nick answered, "I used to work in these mines as a young man. Several years in fact. Still know my way around. We are currently in the iron mines. About a 100 yards there will be another corridor that leads to the silver mines. The miners discovered it while expanding the corridors. There were small traces of silver deep within the exterior layers of rock. Some of which we didn't fully excavate before the closing. We will have protection there. We have to hurry!" Nick Rosalie started to walk forward, but he tripped over a large wooden box and fell to the ground.

Nick cried out, "Ouch! God damn it!"

Mike ran over to Mr. Rosalie and asked, "Are you okay sir? Are you injured?"

Nick answered, "It's my knee! I busted it up when I fell. Tripped on this box here."

Ryan picked up Mr. Rosalie's make-shift torch and looked at the open box. He observed its contents and said, "Whoa! I don't think those are fireworks!"

Nick replied, "Wait! Don't touch that, sonny! And get that damn torch away from the box! I think I know what's inside. Young men, Liam and Mike, help me up if would you please?"

Mike and Liam helped Mr. Rosalie to his feet as he requested. He brought his light over to the box and then examined it contents. He immediately withdrew the fire away from the box, realizing that it was dynamite! Nick addressed everyone saying, "I thought they got rid of this stuff when they closed the mines. This here is dynamite and blasting charges. A few buddies of mine used to be in charge of blasting and expanding the tunnels."

Just then, they heard a loud howl and something large coming down the tunnel from which they entered. It was the werewolf! Liam turned and shined the light from his make-shift torch toward the entrance. The first thing he saw were the two yellow eyes and the beast coming toward them! Liam turned back to his friends and yelled, "Run! Go now!"

They didn't hesitate. They knew that the silver mines were the only way they could possibly be safe from the monster. Rita, Boo, Ryan, and Robert were in front. Nick grabbed some sticks of dynamite from the box. Mike and I helped Mr. Rosalie make haste by running side by side with Mr. Rosalie in the middle. They all ran and fast as they could. The beast was closing in on them quickly. Suddenly, Mr. Rosalie stopped Liam and Mike in their tracks and said, "Liam and Mike, keep going. Remember, just a few more yards and you make it to the silver mines."

Liam said, "No! Please, Mr. Rosalie! Please stay with us! How will we—?"

Nick interrupted, "The silver mine will lead to the surface. Leave me your torch, sonny. Now, go!"

Liam gave Mr. Rosalie and hug as Mike grabbed his hand to move forward saying, "Come on, Liam. Let's go! Now!"

Liam ran quickly to catch up with his friends and Boo. As Liam and Mike were catching up to them, Ryan was in the back of the pack. He kept his torch held high so Mike and Liam could see which way to go. Ryan yelled, "This is it. These are the silver mines!"

Liam and Mike ran up to Ryan, then he asked, "Where's Mr. Rosalie?"

Mike answered, "He's buying us some time. He made his decision. The mine leads to the surface. Go!"

Nick stumbled his way to the entrance of the silver mines. He looked back, and the beast was within a few yards of his position. Nick stumbled a few yards farther into the silver mines and then stood up and looked at the beast. The beast stopped moving as he saw who was standing in front of him. Nick yelled, "Yeah, that's right. You ugly monster. Just you and me. You leave those kids alone!" Nick raised and aimed his weapon.

The beast growled and howled at Nick. The werewolf showed the full display of his teeth as it pointed his deadly claws at him. The beast was about the charge. Nick found his shot and fired! He hit the beast right into the middle of his chest. This was the lethal shot had Nick waited for since the nightmare began all those years ago. Nick stumbled slightly farther into the silver mines. The beast was severely wounded. Blood dripped from his body. The werewolf could no longer be stable on its feet. Nick reloaded his rifle to fire the final shot and end the curse. He quickly reloaded, took aim, and then the beast lunged forward, digging its deadly jaws into Mr. Rosalie's shoulder.

The bite forced Nick's rifle and torch from his hands, and he fell to the floor. His rifle was out of reach. The torch was fairly close by his side. The beast followed Nick down to the floor, and Nick was pinned under the werewolf. Nick reached for the dynamite that he had secured in his jacket pocket and reached with his outstretched arm toward the flame of the torch. Nick knew he was dying. The curse needed to end. He looked at the beast and said, "The curse ends with you and me together, old friend!"

The beast howled as Nick screamed. The beast tried to stand up, but it was no use. The spark from the end of the dynamite quickly made its way to the base. Suddenly, there was a loud *BOOM!* Fire and smoke filled the corridor of the tunnel and rapidly made its way towards the group. Rita held Boo's hand as she raced in front of the pack.

Rita yelled, "Up ahead, I can see light. The glow of the moon! We are almost there!"

Liam, Mike and Ryan could hear the thunderous sounds and vibrations of the tunnel collapsing. Rita and Boo were the first to make it out of the tunnel. Followed by Robert. Ryan was next. Ryan shouted back, "Come on, guys! Almost there! Use those legs!"

Mike and Liam ran as fast as they could through the mines. The walls behind them were beginning to collapse, and the smoke spread rapidly through the tunnel. Mike reached the surface. The smoke was now surpassing Liam as he lost his sense of direction. The velocity and toxic atmosphere of the smoke sent him flying down to the ground. Liam was choking, coughing, and unable to move. Suddenly, a hand reached down, grabbed Liam, and pulled him out into the open air. It was Mike! Liam was on the ground coughing for a few moments trying to catch his breath and collect his thoughts. Liam said, "Thank you, Mike! Truly!"

Mike replied, "No worries, Liam. You would have done the same for me."

Meanwhile, Will, Annie, Jennea, Bobby, and the state trooper already made their way to the reservation and were searching for the group in the wilderness. The state trooper located the flashing lights from Chief Patterson's car. Due to that the smell of the smoke, they were all quickly led to the settlement where they found the carnage of the night's events. Bobby was overcome with emotion. He fell to his knees and began to weep as he looked down at the dead body of Chief Patterson.

The state trooper exclaimed, "Good Lord!" The state trooper quickly checked the victim's vitals, but he knew it was too late. The state trooper said into his radio, "Michigan State 155 to State Police Command. Send as many resources as you can to the wilderness section along the Lake Gogebic area. I have two officers down! Repeat, two officers down! Both were killed in action! We also have multiple victims on scene. Dead on arrival."

Will ran over to Little Red-Eyed Loon and checked to see if he was still alive. Will also knew it was too late.

Annie went over to Will and gave him a big hug. "Will, what are we going to do? Where are our babies? How could they—"

Will interjected, "Annie I'm sure the kids are fine. They are both brave and strong. We will find them!"

Just then, they all heard the loud boom coming from the mines.

There was silence for a few moments. Jennae exclaimed, "What the hell was that?"

Will answered, "I don't know! I hear someone talking loudly over there. A few people. Sounds like Liam. Let's go!"

They all made their way toward the commotion. Within minutes, they were close to the sounds. Will shouted, "Liam! Boo! Kids are you there!"

Jennea yelled out, "Rita, Mike, where are you!"

Mike was the first to hear the shouts and said, "Help! We are over here. Near the exit of the mines!"

The group all began shouting, "We're here! We're here!"

Will, Annie, Jennea, Bobby, and the state trooper found the rest of the group soon enough.

Will and Annie ran toward Boo and Liam and gave them the biggest hugs and kisses ever! Jennea did the same as she embraced her two children.

Bobby exclaimed, "I'm so glad to see you're okay, kids. What the hell happened out here? Was my dad here with Chief Patterson and Wellington?"

Mike answered, "Officer, please, I'll explain. We came out here to get help from the native tribes. The chief officers and Mr. Rosalie found us out here. The chiefs stayed back and defended the area, and your dad led us into the mines for protection. The loud boom you heard was your dad ending the curse of the werewolf. I'm sorry, sir. He's gone!"

Again, Bobby was in disbelief and overcome with emotion. Will walked over to his friend and said, "I'm sorry, Bobby. I am forever grateful to you and your dad for protecting my kids and their friends. I just wish it didn't end like this."

Still sobbing, Bobby replied, "It's okay. In a way I think this is the way my dad wanted to end this story. Seems like he had some unfinished business with the beast, and he wanted to finish it."

Within an hour, the area was illuminated by several helicopters and police search lights. Help arrived from everywhere. The kids were sitting in the back of an ambulance with blankets wrapped around them from the evening chill. They each took turns being examined by the medics. Thankfully most of them made it out with just some cuts and scratches. Liam was given some oxygen and some medication to help clear his lungs from the dust cloud. Ryan went over to Rita and said, "Not too bad of a first date. Maybe next time we just stick to pizza and a movie."

Rita gave Ryan a small kiss on the cheek and said, "You're really cute. Thank you for being so brave. Maybe someday we can have that second date, but I would wager that you're heading back to Chicago at first light."

Mike came over to Liam and said, "You, Boo, and your friends here are pretty brave. Thank you for your help. You should be proud."

Liam answered, "Thank you, Mike. I'm sorry about your grandfather, but now we know what happened. At least we made it out in one piece."

Mike replied, "That's for sure. Maybe if my grandmother doesn't sell the lake house I'll see you next summer."

Will walked over to Liam and Mike overhearing their conversation and said, "I wouldn't plan on it, kid. If I were a betting man, I think your grandparents are going to sell that lake house. Too many bad things have happened here. Plus, your mother and I were talking. No lake house next summer regardless of whether or not your grandparents decide to sell it. Now's let head home. Gather your friends, kid."

Ryan walked with Robert and asked, "So, did this play out like one of your monster movies?"

Robert answered, "Not even close! This was a real story. Usually, I don't feel anything for the characters in those old monster movies. This affected real people. It's sad, but I'm grateful to have made it through safe and sound. I don't think your folks or mine will let Liam's parents take us anywhere anytime soon!"

They both laughed as they made their way into their ride home.

They all entered the car. It was a full boat with Boo, Ryan, Robert, Will, Annie and Liam. Rita and Mike stayed with their mother. Will shouted, "That's enough excitement for one family trip. We are heading back to the lake house to freshen up and then go straight home to Chicago."

Ryan asked, "Sir, can we come hang out with your family next summer? Seems like you all lead an exciting life!"

Will answered, "Unfortunately no, kid. Annie and I were talking, and next summer we are heading to Pennsylvania right outside Philadelphia. I grew up out there. The family will be spending time with their cousins and their auntie Claire and uncle Pete. The family needs to spend time away from the UP. Somewhere safe."

They drove off and back towards Iron River. The sun was beginning to rise. As Liam saw the sun rise in front of them, he felt a sense of peace. Boo was already sleeping. Liam slowly drifted off to sleep. Liam didn't recall too much about that particular sleep, but he knows that he didn't dream of the monster and its two yellow eyes.

THE END

The story continues with the next great adventure of Liam and Boo as they travel east to Pennsylvania in the "Echoes of Elk's Estate."

www.ingramcontent.com/pod-product-compliance
Lightning Source LLC
Chambersburg PA
CBHW071528120726
47907CB00013B/1253